"Now you [   ] your [   ]"

"You're free to get your freak on in each and every room in the house, whenever and however you feel like it without worrying about little, prying eyes," she continued.

"Oh, please, that's the last thing on my mind," Josette told the younger woman, dismissing the idea with a wave of her hand.

"What do you mean the last thing on your mind?" Natalie asked as her eyebrows arched in surprise. "Don't tell me you and Seth are an old married couple who sleeps in separate beds like Ralph and Alice Kramden on the *The Honeymooners?*"

"No, it's not that bad, but…well, wait until you've been married for as long as I have. You'll see what I'm talking about. *Freaky* is no longer a word in my vocabulary," Josette explained, with a wistful sigh….

Books by Kim Shaw

Kimani Romance

Forever, for Always, for Love

Kimani Press Arabesque

Pack Light
Free Verse
Love's Portrait

KIM SHAW

is a high school English teacher in New Jersey and has enjoyed creative writing since she was a child. She resides with her husband and two children, and enjoys reading, volunteering and would like to become a world traveler.

KIM SHAW

*F*OREVER, FOR ALWAYS, FOR LOVE

KIMANI
ROMANCE

 KIMANI PRESS™

ISBN-13: 978-0-373-86007-4
ISBN-10:   0-373-86007-2

FOREVER, FOR ALWAYS, FOR LOVE

www.kimanipress.com

Printed in U.S.A.

Dear Reader,

Many of you who have enjoyed my previous novels have asked me to write a story about the mature woman and her particular struggles. Therefore, I give you Josette Crawford. She is you, she is me...she is every woman. I hope that you thoroughly enjoyed her story and, more important, that you learned from her that life is a continually evolving state of being. Through Josette we were able to see that there is really no such thing as an end; there are only a multitude of beginnings.

Forever, for Always, for Love has a deeply inspired place in my heart. For better and for worse, in sickness and in health, through bad times and good times, Josette and Seth are an inspirational and passionate couple. Thank you for allowing them into your hearts. If you didn't know, now you do—love and romance get better with time! I hope that Seth and Josette inspired you to seek longevity with your mates, taking comfort in the knowledge that you can weather the storms, explore new roads and continue to get *freaked* right into the sunset years.

Please visit my Web site, www.kimshaw.net, for information on upcoming releases. Some of your favorite characters from my prior novels have been itching to get back on the scene, and who am I to deny them fifteen minutes?

Yours truly,

Kim Shaw

Acknowledgments

So here we go again. I'm here at the finish line of another creative work and you, the readers, are right here cheering me on. Thank you so much for understanding that the stories that I have to tell are our stories, yours and mine, and therefore require time and patience to do them justice.

Thank you to Harlequin, my new home, for continuing to seek out love stories which are reflective of the multi-faceted beauty of this world. The stories you help artists bring to life are valuable and necessary.

It is said that people come into your life for a reason and sometimes only for a season. I say no truer words have ever been spoken. Of all the people I have encountered over my lifetime, I can truly say that I have been more blessed than stressed. I have met wonderful people from all walks of life who each, in their own way, taught me something of value. For that I am truly grateful.

Lisa O. Orr, diva extraordinaire. You've been more like a sister than a friend, and I appreciate you having my back.

My sisters and brothers writing, I continue to thank you for the never-ending encouragement, information and advice you give.

Chapter 1

"Marcus? Marcus…did you pack those Clorox wipes I gave you?" Josette yelled to her son as he bounded up the stairs, his size-thirteen Air Force Ones taking two steps at a time.

She closed the lid to the medium-size brown box she was packing on the dining-room table, paused for a moment and then reopened the box. She scanned the contents again, a nagging feeling that she'd forgotten to include something important staying with her and causing her to feel uneasy.

"Marcus?" she shouted again.

"Yeah, Ma, I've got the wipes and the disinfec-

tant and the Glade PlugIns, too," Marcus yelled
from the top of the stairs.

He shook his head and traded a conspiratorial
grin with his father, who was passing him on the
second-floor landing. Father and son were striking
reflections of one another. Tall, athletically built
men, their complexions identical shades—the color
of a brand-new copper penny. Eyes the color of
roasted chestnuts hinted at the virtues of their
humble personalities. Wide, easy smiles lived on
both of their countenances most of the time, even
when they were trying to appear stern. The only
real difference was that Seth's chiseled physique
had begun to soften ever so slightly, rounding out
to reflect his age of forty-seven.

In Marcus, Seth saw himself of twenty-plus
years ago—a hard, young body, lumbering about
with the freedom and agility of youth. Watching his
son now, he was proud to have raised the boy into
manhood and did not feel one ounce of resentment
for what the dual meanings that Marcus's virility
translated into for his own. In fact, it amazed him
that Marcus could be the product of himself. He
believed that he had been a good father. In a day
and age when young men seemed to be struggling
ferociously to establish their identities, being
swayed by too many of the wrong images of what
masculinity meant, Marcus was a refreshing
example of the positives. Seth truly believed that
in many respects, young African-American men

had a much harder way to go than he did. When
Seth had been born in the fifties, he'd been taught
that to be a man you must first watch a man. As he'd
grown up, he'd had all types of men around him to
watch—his father, the fathers of his friends, Mr.
Ned, the man who'd owned the grocery store in
their Harlem neighborhood, and Mr. Phillips, the
principal of his high school. Even Big Lou, the
man who'd owned the pool hall, had been a shining
example of what it took to be a man. They'd all
worked, taken care of their families and had respected women. Mr. Phillips had taught the
students, especially the young black boys, about
men of importance who had come before them.
Who ever heard of a principal coming into the
classroom and assigning research projects? He'd
done that, however, and much more.

Seth's own father, Ernest Crawford, was easily
the biggest influence. He was a man who had
worked with his hands most of his life and had
moved his young, pregnant wife up to New York
from Mississippi because he did not want his child
to be born under the laws of Jim Crow. All of Seth's
life his father had taught him that the black man's
biggest fear and, subsequently, his biggest enemy
was himself. He commanded Seth not to be afraid
of his own power and his own abilities. He also told
him that if he ever took no for an answer when
pursuing his dreams or taking care of his family,
then he would be less than a man. To this date, at

seventy-two years old, the elder Crawford was still taking care of his family, supporting and nursing his ailing wife without complaint. Seth's mother, Betty Ann, needed round-the-clock care due to the kidney disease from which she suffered. Although she had a full-time nurse caring for her, Ernest preferred to take care of all of her personal needs, assisting her with bathing and dressing, cooking her food and helping her eat it. The only assistance Ernest would allow was that he permitted Josette to come by every other weekend to wash Betty Ann's thick hair, grease and massage her scalp, and then braid it. Otherwise, Ernest felt it was his responsibility to take care of her.

Seth had followed his father's wisdom and the example of all the other black men in his life to a T. He'd tried hard to instill those same values in Marcus and even though Marcus's life had been a walk in the park compared to what his ancestors before him had had to endure, the boy had truly learned to appreciate what he'd been given. Seth believed that Marcus had turned out to be the kind of man who never had to look to his peers for acceptance or approval, or to see what was either acceptable or unacceptable. Seth could only feel pride in the fact that he and Josette had raised such a fine man. For him, Marcus's departure into this next phase in his life was cause for nothing but celebration.

Josette closed the box in front of her for the

second time since she'd filled it and made a mental note to go upstairs and check the other two boxes in Marcus's room later on. She'd wait until he went out because she didn't want to be accused of snooping through his things or not trusting him—a teenager's most fierce complaint. God forbid she just wanted to make sure that he had everything he needed for his first experience away from home, not counting summer camp and the visits to her parents' place in California.

Josette remained in the dining room, staring absently out of the bay window on the north wall. She searched the lavender sky for unattainable answers as she wondered where the time had gone. It seemed as if it were only a mere five minutes ago, a day at best, when she and Seth had moved into this magnificent house. The brick-faced center-hall colonial was situated on a full acre of property, bordered by dense woods in the town of Larchmont. This small Westchester County, New York, community had been a haven for young, newly successful couples who were starting out in life. They had been the first African-American family on the block and, despite their initial anxieties, they had been received well. In fact, the friendships they'd developed over the years with their neighbors over card games, dinner parties and barbecues were ones that they cherished.

Their daughter, Simone, had been one and a half years old at the time and Marcus had been just a

bubbly infant who had barely cut his first teeth.
Simone had been a chubby, butter-pecan-complex-
ioned baby who'd been an eager explorer even
then. She had run around the entire house that first
day, wanting to see every nook and cranny. Filled
with the natural curiosity and fascination of a
toddler, she'd worn herself out and fallen asleep on
top of a pile of pillows on the living-room floor.
The memories of how Simone had torn through the
house daily, later dragging her baby brother with
her, were as vivid for Josette as if they were yesterday. This was the only home Marcus had ever
really known, and Josette couldn't believe that now
he was leaving it. Moisture formed in her eyes as
she thought about the fact that this meant that he
was also leaving her.

Seth Crawford approached his wife from
behind. At six feet three inches and a hefty two
hundred and fifty pounds, Seth was still a handsome, rugged-looking man. He had a head full of
curly, jet-black hair, the silver streaks now running
through it here and there only an enhancement to
his attractiveness. Women half his age still fluttered
and fussed when he entered a room, yet he never
seemed to notice. Sometimes, Josette noticed but
she never remarked on it, for it didn't make sense
to bring attention to a fact that obviously didn't
affect her husband one way or another.

He greeted everyone with the same warmth and
sincerity, a trait that had made him the successful

attorney he was today. Seth placed his thick hands on Josette's shoulders, giving them a firm squeeze. He inhaled deeply, the sultry fragrance of his wife even after all of these years still stirring his loins. Lately, he didn't get close enough to enjoy her scent very often, for she was always running here and there, doing this and that. Sometimes at night, when she was fast asleep after a day of doing, he would inch closer to her and lay his head on her pillow, allowing the scent of her to stroke him as he slumbered.

"Relax, honey, you've already given him more than what he needs," he said.

He only meant to reassure her as much as he himself was reassured about the fact that their son would be okay without them.

"Relax? I am relaxed. He'll be the one calling *me* when he realizes that he's missing something, saying, 'Ma, can you…',", Josette snapped.

She knew that she was being hard on Seth, but she was so tired of everyone telling her to relax. She was not uptight. So what if she'd spent the last couple of months shopping, packing and planning for Marcus's departure? She'd been preoccupied ever since the day he'd announced that he'd decided to go to the University of Miami in Florida. She had hoped against all hope that he would join his sister at Stockton College in South Jersey. Alternatively, he had the grades as well as the character and social skills to get into just about any

school to which he wanted to apply and could have
chosen either Princeton or Harvard, both schools
more suitable to Josette's taste due to their closeness to home. However, he'd chosen to go south,
and since she and Seth had raised both of their
children to be independent and follow their own
minds, his decision was nonnegotiable. When
Simone had left for college last year, it hadn't
seemed like as big of a deal. The fact was she
would only be a two-hour drive away from home
and they continued to see her almost as much as
they had when she was in high school. It was
nothing for Simone to drive home on a Tuesday
evening because she needed an outfit out of her
closet or wanted her mother to make her a pan of
her signature eggplant lasagna or crispy fried
chicken. She'd stay over and leave early the next
morning in time to return to classes. Josette was
very happy to accommodate Simone, too. She
always had been.

Josette knew that Seth thought she spoiled the
kids, but she didn't care. She took pride in knowing
that all of her children's needs were met, and it didn't
matter how old they got, nor how far from home they
traveled, she would always be there for them. Marcus
was headed off to a college at the other end of the east
coast, but she wasn't about to send him off unarmed.
She was his mother, and no one could tell her that it
wasn't her duty and her right to make sure that he
would be comfortable in his new surroundings.

Seth didn't reply. He let out a barely audible, defeated sigh, released her shoulders and lumbered away. He knew that no matter what he said, Josette would continue to worry, and she would race about to and fro until the last possible second taking care of their kids. It was what she did best. He mournfully recalled a time when *he* had been the center of her universe, and she'd run around catering to his every desire. They had been married for almost twenty-one years and, while he still loved his wife dearly, he had never expected the burning embers of their love to be replaced by lukewarm companionship. Josette was still a beautiful woman in his eyes. He used to call her his own personal Diahann-Carroll-Lena-Horne. She even had a sexy, jazzy singing voice, which she shared occasionally during family gatherings around the piano, but had mostly saved for late-night seduction in their bedroom in the early days of their union. Now, it was fuzzy slippers and flannel pajamas, along with reading glasses and five-hundred-page novels that greeted him every night. Sometimes it seemed that if she didn't have something related to the kids to talk about or a problem at work plaguing her thoughts, she had nothing else to say to him.

Seth realized that it was his own foolish thinking that was to blame. He had stupidly expected her eyes to continue to light up every time he entered a room and for her to always tuck love notes into his suit-jacket pocket when he left for work in the morning. Those days were long past, but surely not forgotten. Now that their second and last child was leaving home, Seth hoped that some of that attention would finally be refocused on him. He guessed he'd just have to wait and see…and hope.

Josette drummed nervous fingers on top of the box she'd finally closed and taped shut. *What could she be forgetting?* Tomorrow afternoon this time, Marcus and his friend Christian would be in the charcoal-gray Chevy TrailBlazer they'd bought Marcus for his graduation, with a U-Haul wagon hitched to the back, headed south. She had wanted to make the trip with them, but Marcus was adamant about it not being necessary. She masked her feelings of rejection with the knowledge that the truck would be pretty loaded up with both boys' things, anyway, leaving little room for her. She knew that she would not get an ounce of rest until she had received confirmation that he had arrived safely on campus.

Relax? How could she relax? Her eighteen-year-old son was about to drive three thousand miles south into a new life, where he'd be on his own and away from her. It would be December before she got to see him again. That thought alone made her stomach contract. It was easy for Seth to be unfazed by the situation. A father's role in the family was never as intricately interwoven with the children's daily lives as a mother's was. She had done all the day-to-day grunt work, while he strode around like a proud peacock whenever anyone acknowledged what terrific, accomplished children they had. She was the one who had nurtured and raised them from birth to today. She'd taught them how to read before kindergarten, made sure they'd memorized their telephone number and address, and trained them to protect themselves from strangers. She'd slept in their beds with them when chicken pox had struck, rubbing their sores with calamine lotion every twenty minutes and force feeding them liquids to keep them from becoming dehydrated. Her beautiful little babies...all grown up. It was so hard for her to swallow that pill, especially when it came to Marcus. Marcus had been a mama's boy from the moment he'd come into the world. He adored his mother and she him. He'd spent loads of time with her, doing the things that Simone never wanted to do, such as grocery shopping, baking and yard work. *Whatever would she do now?*

She strummed an erratic beat on the box again and sighed. She quickly wiped away the single tear that had formed in her eye, knowing that she could not allow anyone to see how upset she was, especially not Seth. He would never understand. She hurried up the stairs, her French braid slapping against her back lightly, finally remembering what she had forgotten. She moved past their snoozing golden retriever, Lady, who at ten years of age no longer bothered to rouse herself from her slumber

when anyone approached. Josette searched the
medicine cabinet, grateful that she'd finally remembered that she hadn't packed the Pepto-
Bismol she kept on hand by the case for Marcus.
Despite her many warnings, he often ate greasy,
fried fast food and ended up with a belly ache.

Chapter 2

"Earth to Josette. Come in, Josette," Natalie said, waving slender fingers with frosty bronze-painted nails in front of Josette's dreamy face.

"Huh? Oh, Natalie, I'm sorry. Did you say something?" Josette replied.

They were seated in Josette's modest office at New Hope, the nonprofit social-service agency of which she had been the director for the past five years. She had been a stay-at-home mother up until Marcus had entered middle school. At that point, both his and Simone's lives had become so active with school, clubs and sports that she'd found herself left with hours each day in which she had absolutely nothing to do. She had earned her master's degree in social work from UCLA, where she'd met Seth, and had worked for the first couple of years of their marriage for First 5 Association of California, a social-services agency designed to improve the lives of young children and their families. She'd followed Seth to New York—his hometown—where he'd accepted an entry-level associate position at the law firm of Waters, McLean and Berber. She'd fallen in love at first sight with the city and soon shed her little California-girl ways along with her Mexican-American accent.

The product of a union between a Mexican woman, her mother, Lourdes Velazquez, and a black and Seminole man, her father, Benjamin Medwala, Josette was a multicultural people lover. The big melting pot of New York City had been the perfect place for her to get to know the numerous cultures that fascinated her. Seth had taken pleasure in showing her his New York, watching her eyes light up and her breath blow away every time some new and curious spectacle caught her attention. Even when his professional obligations had begun to keep him too busy to be with her, she'd made her way around the five boroughs on her own. She'd volunteered at soup kitchens, public playhouses, churches and hospitals, spreading her cheer and bright spirit anywhere it was needed. She'd soaked in the cacophony of cultures, delighting and amusing herself daily. When Seth would come home after a long day at the office, she would be there waiting with dinner, a back rub, endless tales of her adventures and languid lovemaking.

While Josette had loved working and volunteering, she and Seth both believed that having a parent at home was the most beneficial thing for children. She was a product of day care, having been enrolled from the time she was an infant when her mother had returned to her job at the post office. She'd received her own set of house keys at the age of eight and had later been responsible for her younger brother and sister. Seth was an only child and both of his parents had been laborers. He'd spent many days either at the library or home alone. Admittedly, there'd been times when he'd been very afraid and very lonely, but he'd known that his parents had had to do what they'd had to do to feed the family and keep a roof over their heads.

When their kids had come along, they'd been in perfect agreement and Josette had dived into the role of motherhood with no hesitation and no regrets. They'd just been grateful that Seth made enough money to afford them the opportunities and the liberties that their parents had not had.

Later on, when she'd taken the position at New Hope, the agency had been struggling to keep its doors open. Josette had immediately fallen back in love with being of service to people who needed a new start in life. At New Hope they provided job training for clerical positions, assisted clients in applying for public aid, health-care benefits and other social services, which included, but were not limited to, mortgage services, home energy and heating assistance and assistance with income-tax preparation and small-business ventures. They also partnered with battered women's shelters to assist those women in getting back on their feet, finding child care and places to live.

The New Hope staff was small in number, but big in effort. Along with Natalie Alexander, who was the services coordinator, there was Francesca Ruiz, Donna Thornton and Roman Daniels. Francesca and Roman ran the job-training program, while Donna liaised with public social-service agencies to obtain benefits for New Hope's clients and assist with low-income housing searches.

"Girl, you were a million miles away. What's wrong?" Natalie said, pulling the worn, pea-green armchair in front of Josette's paper-strewn desk closer.

At thirty-five years old, Natalie had become a younger sister to Josette. A tall, slim, natural beauty who could easily have been a cover model, Natalie was equally in love with being of service as Josette. Before coming to New Hope, she had worked for a city agency, but had always felt as though her role put her in the game too late. She wanted to be there when women and their families needed her most, as opposed to when they were at their last resort.

In a field where money was not an incentive, dedicated servants like Josette and Natalie were hard to come by and even harder to keep.

Josette had not cultivated many friendships during her life. Growing up with her siblings, there had always been someone to play with and, therefore, never a real need to seek out other playmates. Her circle of friends was small and by college, they had all grown up and gone their separate ways. The only childhood friend she remained in touch with today was Maribell Munoz, who was now a lieutenant in the United States Army and had been living in Germany for the past ten years. The associations Josette held with other moms whom she'd met through the Parent and Teachers Association of the kids' various schools produced infrequent phone calls and cards during the holidays. There were also their neighbors, with whom Josette and Seth shared barbecues and card games, but those were not close relationships, either. When Josette and Natalie had first met at New Hope, it had been at the right time and they'd just clicked. Josette truly counted her as a dear friend.

Natalie's knee tapped against the oak desk, causing it to shake a bit. One of the legs was uneven, and Josette made a mental note to replace the stabilizing matchbook that must have come dislodged from beneath it. One day she knew that God would have mercy on them and send them the funds to fix up their offices. She knew they were doing the work that needed to be done and would, therefore, be blessed to continue doing it. In the meantime, Josette used her own money from time to time to make enhancements that were absolutely necessary around the place and they made do with what they had, as little as that was.

"Nothing's wrong. I've just got a lot on my mind. The agency that promised me three jobs now says they've only got room for one and at two dollars an hour less than we'd discussed. Plus, Mrs. Parker missed her last two appointments with ACS and the caseworker is pissed off to say the least. I tell you, it just doesn't pay to get out of bed on a Monday, does it?"

"I hear you. I'm all for shutting the doors and starting this day all over again from home," Natalie agreed. "So, did Marcus get off okay?" she asked, changing the subject.

"Yep. He should be somewhere around Georgia right now. I told him to call me this morning, but that boy's got cobwebs where his memory bank is supposed to be," Josette answered, glancing at the Bulova pearlized-diamond wristwatch Seth had bought her for their twentieth anniversary.

She appreciated the fact that she had a man who had good taste when it came to selecting presents for his wife. Over the years he had grown to know what she liked, and usually selected trinkets for her with care and discretion. She knew that she was lucky to have such a wonderful husband, even if she didn't tell him so very often.

"I'll give him until noon before I blow up his cell phone," Josette continued, her thoughts returning to her traveling son.

"Mama Bear's worried, huh?" Natalie laughed.

"Am I that obvious?" Josette asked.

"Yes, but it is more than okay. You've got every right to be worried about your baby boy. Please, my boo is entering first grade next month, and I'm thinking about how many six-year-old butts I'm going to have to go up to that school to kick if they mess with him. I can't imagine what I'll be like when he's heading off to college. Time flies, huh?"

"It sure does. I can't believe he's gone—they're both gone now. It seems like only yesterday when I was packing school lunches and hanging Crayola drawings on my refrigerator," Josette said nostalgically.

"Well, look at it this way. You and Seth have the whole house to yourselves now. You're free to get your freak on in each and every room, whenever and however you feel like it without worrying about little prying eyes!" Natalie laughed.

"Oh, please, that's the last thing on my mind," Josette said, dismissing Natalie with a wave of her hand.

"What do you mean, the *last* thing on your mind?" Natalie asked, her eyebrows arched in stark surprise. "Don't tell me you and Seth are an old married couple who sleep in separate beds like Ralph and Alice Kramden on *The Honeymooners?*"

"No, it's not that bad. But wait until you've been married for as long as I have. You'll see what I'm talking about. *Freaky* will no longer be a word in your vocabulary," Josette advised, believing herself to have dropped sage words of wisdom on her younger colleague.

"Humph. If the day comes when I'm no longer interested in good sex, you might as well dig a hole and bury me, 'cause what's the point?" Natalie laughed, eyeing her friend with skepticism.

As Josette hurried back and forth between the closet and the pile of clothes on her bed, she caught an image of a woman she didn't recognize in the full-length mirror behind the bedroom door. She stopped her mad dash, frozen in her tracks. She turned around to face the mirror and looked at the reflection that stared back at her. In the mirror was a woman who could have been her mother, were she three shades lighter in skin complexion. Josette took a tentative step closer to the glass, cocked her head to the side and then took another small step. She couldn't remember the last time she had looked at herself, had truly studied her image in a mirror, and now that it had been sprung unexpectedly upon her, she was displeased at the picture before her.

When had she gone from a slim, curvaceous vixen to the pudgy, middle-aged woman who stood before her? The ivory-colored brassiere and full briefs she wore made her once-shapely body look matronly. Little wrinkles had formed at the corners of her eyes and around the edges of her lips. Her face was puffy, the extra weight she had picked up over the years having settled there, among other places. The long French braid that hung from her head made her lackluster hair look limp and boring. The only thing polished about her seminude appearance were her manicured finger- and toenails. She had a standing weekly appointment, year-round, at Ms. Yip's House of Nails. But even they were a plain, pale, pink-frosted color over short, squared nails. She had been wearing the same polish for more years than she could count.

She looked like somebody's mother. This was a startling thought that made her both proud and ashamed at the same time. She loved her children more than life itself and loved being their mother, but when had she begun to look like a *mother?* Inside, she felt the same as she had twenty years ago, or at least that was what she'd led herself to believe all these years.

Stunned, she pulled herself away from the mirror, her numb body almost stumbling over to the six-drawer oak chest across the room. She picked up a porcelain-framed photograph of her and Seth, taken last year on a family vacation to

Bermuda. She was wearing a long floral skirt and
a turquoise tank top. Her ever-present French braid
was in place. She had not noticed that standing
next to Seth, she looked plain. Seth had aged well.
His tall, fit physique had picked up a few pounds,
but they only served to make him look like a man
who lived a satisfying life. His mustache was
thicker now than he'd worn it in his youth and, like
his hair, was lightly sprinkled with gray throughout, but otherwise, he had not changed very much.
Seth was a big man who still played basketball
with Marcus a couple of times a week and also rode
his bicycle on Saturday mornings with their neighbor Phil, who lived up the street. Josette used to
ride with them, up until about four or five years
ago. She had become too busy, what with the kids
and work.

    She collapsed onto the edge of the bed, staring
down at the photograph in her hands, her slightly
protruding belly in her direct line of vision. She
sucked her teeth in disgust. She looked around the
bedroom, as if it were her first time in there, and
tried to figure out when time had stopped being her
friend. She remembered when she and Seth had
first found the house. After showing them the entire
home, one of the last of a half-dozen houses built
by a developer on a previously untouched area of
Larchmont, the real estate agent had left them alone
for another appointment. They had fallen in love
with the house from the moment they'd pulled into

the driveway. They'd toured the house on their own all over again, ending up in the master bedroom where they'd made love on the plush tan carpet. Giggling like newlyweds, they'd left the house, called the Realtor's office and made an offer. The house had been theirs a month later.

Josette had decorated the entire house by herself, with little input from Seth, save for an occasional grunt of approval. She had wanted their bedroom to be warm and cozy, a haven for them to rededicate themselves to one another every night after Seth returned from his grueling law practice and she had tucked the children safely into their beds. In the wintertime, she always kept the room's fireplace burning low. She kept satin sheets in various shades of ice-blue, mint-green and buttery-yellow, what she believed to be inviting colors, on their king-size bed. The plush carpet was the kind a person could sink his or her toes into or lie down on whenever passion overtook the senses, which had been often for them back then. She'd taken a class in the art of massage, where she'd learned all kinds of techniques, which she'd used on Seth. The first few years of his career had been difficult. He'd worked long hours, longer than many of his colleagues as he'd proven that he was not only equal to them but even a smarter and craftier adversary in the courtroom. Josette had felt it was her duty every night to rejuvenate her man and prepare him to go back out the next morning and fight for his

place in that firm. The fringe benefits were that
Seth did everything in his power to make her feel
good, loving the ability to bring her to the highest
heights of pleasure even more than getting there
himself. They'd worn one another out frequently.
This bedroom had seen its share of steamy inter-
ludes. If the walls could talk, Josette didn't doubt
what they would have to say now that the fire had
died out—if they could stay awake long enough to
say anything at all.

Chapter 3

"Good afternoon, Mr. Crawford's office," the secretary said.

"Pamela, it's Josette. How's it going?"

"Hello, Josette. Boy, it's a madhouse in here today, I'll tell you. How are you doing?"

"I'm fine and yourself?"

"Fair. Let's just say I'll be doing a whole lot better at five o'clock, if you know what I mean." Pamela laughed.

"I hear you, but try to take it easy. Is my husband free?"

"Hold on a moment for him. He just came back to his office."

"Thanks, Pamela."

Pamela Dawson had been Seth's secretary for the past fifteen years. Josette often joked to her that she was his office wife. Seth readily acknowledged that he could not do his job nearly as well were it not for Pamela's competence and dedication. She was a few years older than Seth and Josette, and despite the fact that he was the superior, he revered her as he would an older sister or aunt. Many of the other secretaries in the law firm felt that Pamela received preferential treatment, but if that was true, she deserved it and Seth would be the first one to go to bat to protect her position there.

Josette breathed into the phone, tapping her foot absently to the bland music that served to entertain the caller while waiting to be connected.

"Hey, honey," Seth said as he snatched up the receiver.

"Hi, dear. How's your day going?"

"Busy. Just had two never-ending conference calls back to back, and I've got a meeting starting in just about five minutes," Seth replied, clicking into his computer's mailbox to check his electronic messages.

"Did you have time for lunch?"

"Aah, I grabbed a sandwich," Seth admitted, knowing that Josette would not be happy to know that he'd actually only eaten one or two bites of that sandwich, since she had him on a very strict regimen of nutrition. "It's been murder around here today. Everybody's nervous because the RESCO deal fell through," Seth said as he sifted through a stack of papers in search of a document he needed for his meeting.

Seth's office was immaculate. He was very organized, especially when it came to his business affairs. He kept working files for each active case and could usually put his fingers on whatever he needed at a moment's notice. He found the document he needed and prepared to head downstairs to the conference-room floor for his meeting.

"Oh, no, Seth. I'm sorry to hear that," Josette offered.

She knew that this was a major setback for one of Seth's biggest clients. They had been working around the clock on that merger for the past couple of months. Even though she knew that this was a difficult blow, she also had faith that Seth would somehow manage to steer things in the right direction eventually. He was a pro at smoothing rough terrain.

"All right, well, I won't keep you," Josette said.

"No, no. Tell me, what's up?" Seth asked.

He'd picked up on the note of distress in his wife's tone. She rarely called him at the office, unless it was something that couldn't wait until he got home. He knew she had to have a good reason to be calling now.

It had been over a week since Marcus had started college. Seth had given Josette her space as she'd moped around the house looking as if she'd lost her best friend. Despite how ridiculous it seemed to him, he didn't say a word about it for fear of evoking her annoyance again. He'd been hoping that her sour mood would lift soon, and maybe her impromptu phone call was a sign that she was in better spirits. Maybe, if he was lucky, they'd be able to get in some quality time tonight. Lord knows it had been long enough since she'd touched him in more than a passing gesture, such as a pat on the back or a quick hug.

"Well, I was wondering if you were working late tonight or planning to come home in time for dinner," she asked.

"I could be home for dinner, if you want. What are you making?" Seth asked, excited by the possibility of a candlelight dinner like he used to find waiting for him after a long day at the office.

Josette rolled her eyes up in the air. Of course, he'd be thinking about his stomach.

"Actually, I was planning to go out for the evening…with friends… I guess I could make you something before I leave…or there's leftover tuna casserole," she answered hesitantly.

She immediately felt as if she were being a bad wife by making plans that would take her away from home at dinnertime, and was about to take her words back and cancel her plans.

"No, no…uh, don't change your plans. Go…and, uh, have a good time. I could really stay and get some work done," Seth said, trying to hide his disappointment.

Seth hung up and sat back in his chair dumbfounded. He racked his brain to think of the last time Josette had gone out with friends. *Go where?* A familiar pang of jealousy invaded his chest as he realized just how much he was aching for his wife's attention. Once again he had gotten his hopes up only to be disappointed.

"Okay, Natalie, I don't know how I let you talk me into this, but I'm telling you right now…I'd better not get hurt," Josette said.

"Josette, would you stop being such a worrywart and come on and have some fun. All you have to do is relax and do what Mama Sa tells you. Trust me, just follow the lead of the people up in the front lines, and you'll be fine," Natalie reassured her.

Josette and Natalie were in the back row of one of the four spacious classrooms at Dyobi Dance Studios in Manhattan. Josette was dressed in gray leggings and a white T-shirt. The room was filled with about twenty women of varying ages, sizes and ethnicities. In fact, the only place Josette could recall ever having seen so many different types of women meeting together was at a nail salon. Some of them, like Josette, were dressed in gym attire, but most wore colorful sarongs and bodysuits. The thing they had in common was that, with the exception of Josette, they all wore an excited, eager expression on their faces. On the contrary, Josette looked more like a five-year-old on the first day at kindergarten.

Three young men and one older, distinguished-looking man with long, graying dreadlocks were seated on stools in the far corner of the room. They each had a drum in front of them and were warming up, beating out different rhythms and chatting among themselves. Standing with them was a woman who talked excitedly, using hand gestures to make her points to the older man, the lead drummer. The front wall of the room was covered from floor to ceiling by mirrors. Huge, circular light fixtures hung from the high ceiling, bathing the room in stark white light.

Natalie exchanged greetings with a few of the women. Most of them seemed to be regulars like her, who had been taking classes at Dyobi for the past two years. About five minutes after they had arrived, the teacher moved to the front in the center of the class-room and introduced herself as Mama Sa, a native of Senegal. She was about the same age as Josette, yet her full figure was well-toned and shapely. She wore her hair in a short natural, little bits of gray sprinkled about. Her coffee-brown skin shone like rich silk and when she smiled, a wide, pearly white smile through thick lips with a gold cap on her right eyetooth, her eyes seemed delirious with merriment.

Mama Sa led the women in a sequence of warm-ups first. She took them through a series of exercises that stretched their limbs slowly, allowing them to become warm and pliable. Josette followed along, her nervousness slowly dissipating as she found herself able to keep up with ease. Just when she became comfortable with herself, the drummers chimed in with a slow, somber rhythm and Mama Sa began to roll her hips from side to side. With renewed anxiety, Josette looked at the women around her, moving and gyrating, smiles radiating from their faces as if they relished this newfound freedom of movement. Seeing women move about, unabashedly exuding their femininity, did something to her. It brought to mind the words of Maya Angelou's poem, "Phenomenal Woman," in which the beauty of a woman—her thighs, her size and everything else about her—is celebrated in her own words by herself. Josette concentrated on the rhythmic beat of the drums and the sound of Mama Sa's voice, like running water over a wall of rocks; time and space faded away as she emptied her mind of all the inhibitions that had taken root and grown within over the past few years. She allowed her body to move to the drummers' beat as if she were not a rigid, fortysomething-year-old wife, mother of two and effective social-services provider, but merely a woman—glorious, sexy and sensual. That woman hidden within was not carrying an extra twenty pounds, had not lost touch with her husband and did not worry about whether her children would forget about her as they forged their own ways in the world.

For a delicious hour, she glided in bare feet across wood floors, she chanted in answer when the drummers called out to the dancers, and, most importantly, she enjoyed being just Josette, the girl-child turned woman. For that hour she forgot the dull ache that lived within her for her children now turned adults. She was even able to erase the fears she had for the rest of her life and for her marriage. With each drumbeat, each step, she soared.

By the time Josette came down, it was as if something had taken flight within her. That thing was the stuff that self-doubt and hesitation were born from. She felt as though she had just returned from a long vacation and while she had enjoyed her time immensely, she was thrilled to be back at home again. She said hello to her Josette, the woman who had been hiding behind obligations and responsibilities. She shook hands with the inner person who didn't always put her own needs before those of other people whom she'd come to care for or even strangers whom she came into contact with in her job and life. Those people may have needed a helping hand and hers was always stretched out to give. Unfortunately, Josette had lost the ability to balance that giving so that she kept a little bit to give to herself.

"You look like you have discovered the secret of life," Natalie remarked in response to the look of sheer satisfaction Josette wore as they wiped the perspiration from their faces, neck and arms.

"That was amazing," Josette said.

Even though her limbs were already growing sore and would probably ache like hell tomorrow, she felt as though it were worth every minute. At home that evening, she took a bubble bath, setting the water as hot as she could stand it and filling the tub with vanilla-scented bath soap and sea salts. Seth came in shortly after she'd finished dressing for bed. She was seated at the kitchen counter talking to Marcus on the phone. She had two of their largest and oldest photograph albums laid out in front of her.

"Here's your father now. If you need any more information about his side of the family than what I told you, you'll have to talk to him," she said.

Seth leaned down and kissed Josette's forehead.

"What's going on? Who is that?" he asked.

"Your son. He's got a term paper to write on the subject of racial purity and he's using our *mixed-up* family, as he called us, as his case study."

"Mixed-up? That's your side of the family that's all mixed-up. My side is straight. One hundred percent Mandigo," Seth said, smacking his chest twice sharply.

"Oh, please. On that note…all right, Marcus. I'll talk to you later. Okay, I'll tell him. 'Night, son."

Josette hung up the phone.

"Crazy man, your son said he'll call you at the office if he needs more information. I'm going to send him this stack of photographs tomorrow," she said, pointing to a dozen or so pictures to her left.

"What's this paper all about?" Seth asked, placing his briefcase on the floor next to the counter.

He opened the refrigerator and removed the leftover tuna casserole from the night before.

Josette filled him in on Marcus's paper, his first substantial writing assignment of the semester. She was happy to see that he was taking his studies so seriously right from the start and, even though she was not surprised because he had always been a conscientious student, she had to admit that she'd been concerned about his being able to prioritize. College freshmen often fell victim to the freedom and abundance of activities and found themselves slipping behind in their responsibilities.

Seth and Josette had always given their children a complete recounting of their family history and their heritage. From the time the children were little, they'd wanted Simone and Marcus to know who they were and where they came from. Tonight, Marcus had wanted to check some facts of different strings of information he'd already known. Together, they'd conducted a three-way conversation with Josette's mother as many of his questions related to her Mexican roots. By the time they'd finished talking to her, almost an hour had passed and she had retold some of the stories Josette had grown up on, including the one about Josette's grandfather, who'd brought his family to America in 1945 with no possessions and seventy-two cents in his pockets.

It warmed Josette's heart to be able to tell those stories of family strength and endurance to her son. More importantly, she was proud of the fact that her son marveled at hearing about his heritage, especially in a time when young people seemed so disconnected from their ancestors. It reinforced to Josette that despite the fact that her son was far away from her daily influence, she and Seth had laid a foundation on which he would continue to build a bright and responsible future.

Chapter 4

One Saturday shortly after she'd discovered her love of African dance at Dyobi's, Josette gave in to the pressure from Natalie to try something different with her hair. She wanted to just slap herself silly for even mentioning to Natalie that she was feeling bored with her old hairstyle. It was as if Natalie had just been biding her time and waiting for the green light. She made an appointment for them both with her own stylist at a shop uptown in Harlem, on the corner of Malcolm X Boulevard and 133rd Street.

From the moment they walked in, Josette remembered why she had stopped going to hair salons in the first place. The small, cramped store was packed wall-to-wall with women waiting to be done. There was not an empty chair in the place and there were several women standing as they waited to be serviced.

"Uh-uh, Natalie. We're going to be here all day," Josette grumbled as Natalie pushed her inside.

"No, we won't. Maxine knows I don't play that. Come on."

The waiting area of the salon was about two hundred square feet. The white stucco walls were plastered with framed color photographs of women with a wide variety of hairstyles. Many of the styles were elaborate and not at all practical for everyday use, but were amazing to look at all the same. There were about fifteen tan plastic seats positioned around the area, a water cooler in one corner and directly across from that was a magazine rack filled with hair magazines as well as other periodicals ranging from *Time* magazine to *Essence*.

Natalie slid and shimmied her way through the sea of bodies toward the back, with Josette following close behind. A short, heavyset woman with a head full of micro-box braids was standing in the back next to the microwave, eating from a plastic bowl. Her braids, dark at the roots and cherry-red at the ends, contrasted against her dark brown skin. She waved as they approached.

"Hey, girl, what's good?" she said to Natalie.

Natalie leaned over and hugged the woman.

"Hey, Maxine. I'm doing well. How's that baby?" Natalie asked.

"Fat. That boy can eat. Gets it from his mama, I guess," Maxine said, her laughter coming out as a loud gurgling noise.

"Ain't nothing wrong with a fat baby. I bet you any amount of money he's the happiest little thing. Maxine, I'd like you to meet my friend, Josette. She's the one I was telling you about," Natalie said.

Josette shot Natalie a look, wondering what exactly she had been telling this Maxine person about her.

"Hello, Maxine. Nice to meet you," Josette said.

"You, too, Miss Josette. Uh-huh, I see exactly what you mean," Maxine said as she eyed Josette's hair.

Josette touched her ever-present French braid nervously.

"Uh, what are we talking about?" she asked suspiciously.

"Oh, don't worry, honey. Natalie here just told me that you…uh, haven't come up out that braid in the past five years. But don't you worry, we're gonna fix you up right pretty. You can just say goodbye to that tired old braid," Maxine said, scraping the remnants of the meal she'd been eating, which appeared to be some type of meat with brown rice, into the trash can. She sidled over to the sink on the other side of the makeshift kitchen and washed her hands. She returned to

Josette, reached up and ran her wet hand across the top of Josette's head.

"Got you a head full of pretty hair, too, and wanna keep it all tied up like that. Don't make no sense. What you got, some Native American in your family?" Maxine asked as she led Josette to her chair.

She draped a cape around Josette's shoulders.

"As a matter of fact, my mom is Mexican and my father is black and Seminole," she answered.

"Oh, so you're mixed. I can tell," she said as if she were an authority. "Let me see this hair of yours," she said as she combed out Josette's braid.

Maxine spent the next few minutes running her fingers and the comb through Josette's hair, parting it and looking at her scalp and roots. Just when it started to feel good, she stopped.

"Got you a good, strong grade of hair. You don't treat this with anything do you?"

"Uh…no. I mean, I use some cholesterol every now and then, if that's what you mean."

"No perms or texturizers, right?"

"No, none of that. I don't want to be bothered with anything like that. I mean, if you just give it a good wash and set, I think that's enough for today."

Natalie glanced up from the seat she'd found across from them. She raised her eyebrows at Maxine, who smiled conspiratorially behind Josette's head.

"Don't worry, darling. I've got you covered. You just sit back and relax and leave this to me."

Maxine spent the next three hours working alternately on Josette's and Natalie's heads. Josette sat back and relaxed as instructed, resigning herself to the fact that Natalie and Maxine were not going to let her out of that shop without a new look.

The cast of characters who breezed through the salon that day reminded Josette of how colorful black folks could be. There was a never-ending stream of gossiping and laughter, as women sat among virtual strangers and shared everything from their quarrels with the men in their lives to their secret desires about slapping their bosses. They laughed over their kids' dramas and wiped away tears when they talked about their ailing elderly parents. Josette wondered why people spent thousands of dollars on psychiatrists when all they really needed was a good hair washing at their neighborhood salon. She laughed until her sides ached and the hours flew by. As reluctant as she had been to sit down in the first place, listening to the other women gave her a change of heart. When Maxine finally finished, Josette was glad that she had allowed her friend to force her into that chair.

"Oh, my goodness. Look at that," she exclaimed as she gazed into the hand mirror Maxine held behind her and the large wall mirror in front of her.

"Girl, you are fine. Somebody's gonna mistake you for Vanessa Williams if you ain't careful," Maxine exclaimed.

"Oh, Josette. You look absolutely beautiful," Natalie chimed in.

The stylist next to them nodded in agreement.

Maxine had added a dark brown rinse to Josette's hair and then lightened it with blond highlights. She'd washed and conditioned it with a moisturizing treatment system and then blown the hair bone-straight. She'd cut it in layers so that it framed Josette's face and hung down to the center of her back. Josette felt like a very different person from the plain woman who had walked into the salon that morning.

"Maxine, this is fabulous. Oh, I can't thank you enough," Josette said, beaming.

"Girl, if you want to thank me, you will promise me that you will never, ever tie up that beautiful head of hair of yours into that nasty-looking braid again. You hear me?" Maxine scolded.

Josette hugged the woman, who chuckled her loud, cackling laugh again and added Josette's name to her appointment book for two weeks from today. It was amazing what a new hairdo could do for a woman. Josette bounced out of that salon onto Malcolm X Boulevard with a spring in her step that she hadn't had in years. For her, this was the shot in the arm she needed. Unfortunately, Natalie was not quite done with her yet.

"What now?" she cried as Natalie hailed a taxi and pushed her inside.

They drove downtown to Fifty-sixth Street. Josette flipped her hair over her shoulder from time to time, loving the feel and the smell of it as it moved. When they arrived at the Face Time spa, which was located in an apartment building right off Lexington Avenue, Natalie unveiled her surprise. Unbeknownst to Josette, Natalie had made appointments for them to have a full body massage and facial.

The owner, Gabrielle Edwards, was a tall, exotic brown beauty who had been in the skin-care business for over two decades. She took one look at Josette's skin and almost lost her mind.

"What have you been doing with yourself?" she cried.

Josette felt like a little girl who'd been caught gorging herself on forbidden chocolates and carbonated soda, the two things her mother had rarely allowed her to have as a child.

Josette received an informative crash course in skin care. Gabrielle described the damage weather changes caused on black skin, from winter's drying effects to the virtual frying of skin caused by too much fun in the sun.

"Sweetie, black skin is the most resilient, beautiful skin in the world, but if you don't treat it right and pamper it, it, too, will crack," Gabrielle chided her.

"Yes, ma'am," Josette said, even though the woman was not much older than her.

The next couple of hours were spent scraping years of mistreatment and neglect from Josette's skin. The technician assigned to service her today used firm hands to mold and manipulate Josette's body. Her touch became soft and gentle when it came to the skin on Josette's face. To the untrained eye, Josette's skin didn't look bad. She didn't take any special care of it and never had any specific beauty regimens that she followed. However, it had retained some of its youth and elasticity despite that. Gabrielle had recommended a glycolic peel in order to exfoliate Josette's face and since she was comfortable and relaxed, she decided to go for it all. Soft, soothing jazz tunes played in the little room where Josette lay being worked on. By the time she climbed off the table, she felt ten pounds lighter and, although her face felt a little tender in places, she could not believe how vibrant her skin looked and felt. She touched her arms and neck, marveling at the softness that had emerged from beneath the exterior. Josette realized that she had been cheating herself for years. Taking care of other people had somehow translated into not taking care of herself. She didn't understand why she had done that, but vowed that she would never neglect herself again—neither mind, body nor soul.

Josette was so impressed with Gabrielle and her staff, not to mention the soothing ambience of the entire place, that she bought a truckload of products from the spa. To show the gratitude she felt for her friend, who had sprung this whole day of heavenly renewal on her, she insisted on paying for her products, too.

Chapter 5

"I think Seth is having an affair," Josette said, her voice unnaturally high-pitched.

She glanced furtively at Bernardo, a nervous smile on her pouty lips. Her eyes anxiously searched his face, wanting desperately for him to tell her that she was being ridiculous and to shed some light on the mystery that is manhood. Every woman needed to have access to the man's perspective and that source could not be simply the man she was involved with romantically. She needed an objective window through which to look from time to time to shed light on the peculiarities of men. Bernardo, Josette's younger brother, was just that for her. Although she didn't usually come out and ask him directly for his point of view, she did use him, his experiences and his predicaments as a case study of sorts. She learned from him even when all she did was silently observe. She hoped that whatever advice he gave her now, she would be able to believe and use it to cast aside her fears.

"Okay, that one came in from way out in left field. What gives?" Bernardo exclaimed.

To say that Bernardo was surprised by his sister's candid announcement would be an understatement. He was, in fact, shocked. Josette was the most even-keeled, on-point person he knew. Her life was balanced and ordered—perfect kids, solid marriage, career, house and the dog. Nothing was ever wrong with Josette or her family, and Bernardo for one had become dependent on her stability. When they'd met for their customary monthly lunch that day, the last thing he'd expected as he slurped his frozen margarita was to hear that there was trouble in paradise. Seth and Josette were his hope and cornerstone for marriage. If he ever dared to take that plunge, he hoped to have learned enough by watching them to have a successful union of his own with the longevity they had achieved.

They were seated in a booth at the back of Tia Marie, a small Mexican pub in the heart of downtown Manhattan. It was a basement restaurant, which patrons had to enter after descending down six steep

stairs and stooping below the five-foot-seven-inch
door frame. Tia Marie herself greeted her customers
at the door. She was a small woman with a round
waist and ample bosom. Dressed decoratively at all
times in long, flowing, flowery peasant skirts and
billowy blouses, her shiny black hair hung down to
the center of her back. Tia Marie was every Mexican
mother. Bangles jingled on both arms as she shook
people's hands heartily, ushering them to the table
of their own choosing, genuinely happy that they
came in to dine with her. Bernardo loved coming
there and that had nothing to do with the fact that he
had an on-and-off relationship with Tia Marie's
beautiful twenty-five-year-old daughter, Adriana.

"I don't know...I mean...I don't know anything
for sure. I just... It's just—" she stammered, feeling
silly now because she was unable to express vocally
the words that had taken up residence in her brain.

"Come on, Josette. Spit it out. Why do you think
Seth is cheating on you?"

Josette sighed heavily. She considered her
brother's questioning countenance and wished that
she hadn't said anything at all. She hadn't intended
to speak on her suspicions, but for some reason,
seated across from her brother, working on her
second Long Island iced tea, the words had just
jumped from her brain directly out of her mouth.
Now it was too late to take them back.

"I just realized that we haven't had sex in three
months," she whispered.

"Whoa, hey… That's way too much information for me, sis. I mean, come on!" Bernardo exclaimed.

"I'm serious, Nardo. It's like we're roommates instead of husband and wife. I don't know what happened," Josette whined.

"Okay, hold on for one minute," Bernardo said.

He took a huge swallow from his glass as if he'd really needed that, the frosty beverage coursing harshly down his throat. He pushed the plate of stuffed potato skins away from him, clasped his hands in front of himself and stared at his sister.

"Okay…now. Not that I would know this from personal experience, but isn't it true that all marriages experience a decrease in sexual activity over the years? I'm sure I saw that on *Oprah* or *Dr. Phil* or somebody."

"Yeah, but…it's not just that. I mean, it's been years since we were hot and heavy like when we first met. I don't know when things changed. I just woke up one day and realized that we had settled into this comfortable, old-people kind of routine. But the other day I was thinking… I'm only forty-six years old. I'm not an old person. You hear all the time, on those very talk shows you mentioned, that people my age are still swinging from the rafters, and me, I'm like somebody's doddering old grandmother. No wonder Seth doesn't want to touch me!"

"Sis, it sounds to me like you're jumping to some pretty far-fetched conclusions. Just because you and Seth aren't doing the do as often as you used to, doesn't mean the man is having an affair," Bernardo said as reassuringly as he could.

"Well, it definitely means something. Last night, I called myself trying to stoke the fires, so to speak. I cooked his favorite—pot roast and potatoes— chilled a bottle of wine and lit some candles."

"Pot roast? Oooh, yeah…way to tantalize the taste buds," Bernardo said sarcastically.

Josette shot him a stern warning glance. Bernardo signaled to the waitress that he needed a refill by nodding and tapping his now-empty glass.

"Continue," he said.

"Do you know what he did? He goes, 'Oh, babe, everything looks great.' Then he took his plate and went into the den to watch the game. Can you believe that?"

"Well, Josie, where does he normally eat his dinner?"

"In the den, in front of the television. But Nardo, that isn't the point. How could he do that after all the trouble I went to?"

Bernardo pursed his lips and considered his sister's hurt expression.

"Uh, sis, do you think maybe you could have told him that you'd like to have dinner at the table with him? I mean, maybe he just didn't know," Bernardo said gently.

"Didn't know? How could he not know? Candles…wine? I mean, really. You'd have to be deaf, dumb and blind not to know that I was trying to set a mood."

Their waitress approached, bringing another margarita for Bernardo. He took a generous sip before he spoke again.

"Josette, listen—"

"No, Bernardo. Don't try to defend him. I should have known you'd take his side. That's a man for you," Josette huffed.

Bernardo was ten years younger than Josette and, thus far, a confirmed bachelor. He had not had a serious relationship with a woman that lasted more than a year and that was fine with him. He had already seen too many of his friends' marriages end in bitter divorce and had decided that at the ripe old age of thirty-six, he was too set in his ways to adapt to married life anytime soon. Bernardo's work as a translator took him to various parts of the world for extended periods of time. He'd just recently returned from a month's stay in Portugal. Before that it had been England and before that, Turkey. Bernardo loved his job, and he loved to travel. A striking man with evident sultry Latino and dominant African-American features, he had an abundance of female companionship wherever his plane landed. He was extremely frank with every woman he dealt with and offered them as much as he could of himself. His charm and disarming good looks forced many of them to take what he offered, with no hope of permanency, for as long as they could get it. Josette chided herself for even broaching the subject with him. Brother or not, men always stuck together.

"Come on, Josie, don't be like that. I'm not defending him. I'm just wondering if maybe your seduction skills are a little rusty. Maybe you didn't put the vibe out there in the right way. Instead of thinking that he doesn't want you or that he wants somebody else, could it be possible your signal just went way over his head? You yourself said that it's been a minute. Maybe the man just did not get it."

Josette sat quietly in her seat, biting her bottom lip. She'd hate to think that Bernardo was right and that she had lost her touch. That would simply underscore what a mess she had become. How could she have forgotten how to turn her man on?

Bernardo read her mind. He reached out across the table and took her hands in his.

"Listen, big sister, aren't you the one who always says that a person should only stop learning when they're dead? Don't you make it a point to frequently attend seminars and conferences related to social and community services?"

"What does that have to do with this?" Josette asked suspiciously. "Are you suggesting I go back to sex education one-zero-one with the accompanying lab?" She laughed.

"That's exactly what I'm suggesting," Bernardo smiled, a devious twinkle in his eyes.

He pulled out his cell phone and dialed a number from the phone book. Josette shook her head, certain that whatever Bernardo was setting up would be something she'd regret. He silenced her protests with a finger pressed to her lips.

"Trust me," was what he whispered just before the party he was trying to reach picked up the line.

Those two little words were enough for Josette to know that she'd either end up injured or embarrassed if she messed around with her little brother—the same guy who once, when she was sixteen and he six, had gift-wrapped a dead lizard and presented it to her. He'd told her that it was a surprise left by a secret admirer, and she'd been gullible enough to open it up excitedly in front of friends. After she'd tripped and fallen, spraining her ankle as she'd tried to get away from it, she'd nearly died of embarrassment as her friends had laughed hysterically at her.

However, at this stage, she felt as if she had to take the risk. Hopefully, her brother had outgrown childish pranks and would actually be able to offer her some constructive assistance. If not, she'd enjoy killing him after a slow, torturous beat-down.

Chapter 6

One week after her alcohol-aided lunchtime confession to Bernardo, Josette found herself seated on an overstuffed, red-velvet-covered bean-bag chair close to the white-shag-carpeted floor in the darkened, incense-filled office of Dr. Olivia Turnup. The doctor had a successful practice as a marriage counselor and sex therapist in lower Manhattan. Josette stared at Dr. Turnup with wide-eyed astonishment as the woman, old enough to be her mother, questioned her about her ability to reach orgasm.

The call Bernardo had made was to a woman friend of his who worked as Dr. Turnup's secretary.

According to his friend, Dr. Turnup was the best in the field and could successfully turn a grandmother into a pole-dancing sex kitten. Josette had assured Bernardo that the last thing she wanted was to learn pole tricks, but she'd gone along with it after a sufficient amount of arm twisting.

"Well, uh...uh," Josette stammered, her face flushed with embarrassment.

"Josette, dear, there is nothing to be embarrassed about. Unfortunately, we women have a historical legacy of self-denial and suppressed sexual expression. African-American women in particular have been made to feel ashamed, secretive and guilty about our sexuality. It's part of the chains of slavery when our African mothers were abused and misused for the pleasure and gain of the slave master. It made us feel ashamed and dirty and we've carried that internalized disgrace about ourselves and our sexuality for generations. We've passed it down to our daughters along with hand-sewn quilts and recipes."

Dr. Turnup's voice was practical and soothing, despite the harsh words she'd spoken. Josette could not argue with her because her words were similar to conversations she'd had with girlfriends over the years.

"The first step in healing ourselves and our relationships is to let go of that shame and talk freely about what we want and what we need," Dr. Turnup concluded.

"Okay, Dr. Turnup. I hear what you're saying and I honestly don't think I'm suppressed about my sexuality. I just…well, I just didn't expect this," she said, waving her hands in a circular motion to encompass everything, including the room, the doctor and her question.

"Fair enough. Why don't we just start with why you're here then." Dr. Turnup smiled, her face the epitome of patience.

She wore a look that said she dealt with women like Josette all the time—women who showed up at her office claiming to be completely perfect, but whose insecurities were as transparent as Plexiglas.

"Fine. You see, my brother and I were having a conversation… Well, I let him talk me into this. I'm not sure why I'm here exactly." Josette sighed.

Dr. Turnup did not speak. She merely continued smiling at Josette, waiting for her to continue. Josette's brain scrambled as she tried to put her thoughts into intelligible sentences that wouldn't turn her own cheeks a deeper shade of red.

"See, I was telling Bernardo—he's my brother. Anyway, I was telling him that it had been some time since my husband, his name is Seth…since my husband and I, well, you know, since we made love," Josette said, whispering the last part conspiratorially.

"I see. What would you categorize as *some time* exactly?"

"Well, a couple…three months," Josette admitted. "I mean, but, you know, we're a busy couple. Seth has a thriving law practice and I, well, you know, with my work at the center and the kids…we sometimes barely get a chance to see each other before we tumble into bed."

"And how does that make you feel?" Dr. Turnup asked.

"Feel? How does what make me feel?" Josette asked.

What kind of stupid quack asks a question like that? Josette wanted to scream that she wasn't *feeling* anything at all, which was precisely the problem.

"How does the fact that you and your husband don't have time to make love make you feel?"

"Feel?" Josette repeated. "Well, I guess it makes me… I don't know."

"Yes, I think you do know," Dr. Turnup stated plainly.

"Well, I guess it makes me sort of wonder if, well, you know. I kind of told Bernardo that I thought that maybe Seth was seeing someone else."

"Oh, so you figure that if he isn't eating at home, he's got to be eating somewhere else?"

Josette gasped, surprised by the doctor's candid statement as well as embarrassed by how accurately she was able to read Josette's thoughts.

"Listen to me carefully, Josette. You are not the first woman in the world to have that thought. You are also not the first woman in the world to be experiencing the frustrations that you are experiencing. You are a woman of mature age, good health and you've been in a committed relationship with the same man for two decades. It is natural for you to want to make love to your husband and when that's not happening, our first instinct is to suspect hanky-panky."

"I don't really believe that Seth is cheating on me. I mean, Seth's a good man. He's a good husband, a good father and has always provided for us," Josette defended.

"I don't doubt that he is all of those things and more. Now, if all indicators conclude that Seth isn't the problem, what do you think it is?"

Josette opened her mouth to respond, but closed it again. She had no answer for the doctor because she didn't know what was wrong. She didn't know what had happened to change the previous rabbit-in-heat nature of their relationship to what it was today. She adored Seth. He was the best thing that had ever happened to her in her entire life, besides her children, and she knew he loved her. Sometimes all she had to do was look at him and tears would come to her eyes at the thought that he was hers. He was an amazing man whose heart was pure, twenty-four karat gold. He was a strong black man who wore his heritage and cultural identity with pride and integrity, never compromising himself for any reason. That made him so attractive and lovable to her. She began to reason that maybe this was how things between a husband and wife were supposed to be in life's later years. Maybe their relationship was in the exact position it was supposed to be in, and she was being greedy to expect more.

As if reading her mind again, Dr. Turnup put a dent in Josette's theory.

"Josette, the passion and fire you felt for your husband when you first met him should follow you to your grave. Barring health concerns, I know couples who are well into their eighties and who have very active, fulfilling sex lives."

"Wow," Josette exclaimed.

She hadn't ever really thought about what her golden years would be like with Seth, but now that she was on the doorstep of the middle portion of her life, it was something to be considered. If the passion and fire, as Dr. Turnup had put it, could be expected to continue blazing, what was wrong with them? Why had theirs turned into ash?

"I assure you it is very possible, but just like everything else, it takes work. A lot of couples spend years learning how to communicate with one another effectively, learning how to share, to compromise and to trust each other. All of those things comprise an important element in the marriage and they are the first things your pastor, priest or even grandma may have counseled you about when you were planning to marry. However, there is another, equally important element that is sometimes over-looked—that is how to satisfy one another and our-selves sexually on a continuous basis."

"No, Grandma certainly didn't talk about that." Josette laughed.

"That's because we try to pretend that people get married solely for the purpose of companionship and to raise a family. But isn't part of the beauty of marriage having someone you can go home to and get your boots rocked on a regular basis?"

Josette blushed and she nodded, recognizing that the doctor had a very good point. She and Seth couldn't keep their hands off of one another back in the old days. She'd been raised in a Christian household, and she'd been very upfront with him about her intentions of remaining a virgin until her wedding night. He had been patient and under-standing, and outside of some heavy petting, there had been no sexual intercourse before their marriage. That first night had been a magical release of months of pent-up desires and wanting.

"So the real question is how do you, as a woman and a wife, keep your man turned on? Conversely, how does a man keep his woman turned on? These need to be concentrated efforts so that both of you can receive the physical, mental and emotional gratification that a human being needs to survive and to thrive."

At the end of a forty-five-minute counseling session, Josette floated from Dr. Turnup's Park

Avenue building in a daze. Armed with Dr. Turnup's book, titled *Honey, You Still Light My Fire,* and a homework assignment to read the book and answer the questions at the end before next week's session, Josette made her way back to New Hope with her mind reeling. Once inside of her office, she shut the door and read the first few pages of the book. It was full of interesting facts about the biological aspects of humans, including scientific explanations of hormones, libido and sexual stimulation. Dr. Turnup's signature wit and humor were as evident in her written work as they were in conversation, thus giving her book a warm, relatable appeal.

Startled by a knock at the door, she tossed the book into a drawer, feeling as guilty as an adolescent girl caught reading one of her mother's steamy romance novels.

"Come in," she called.

Natalie stuck her head in the door, smiling.

"Hey, how'd everything go at the dentist's?" she asked.

"Huh? The dentist… Oh, yes, everything's fine. Couldn't be better," Josette said, trying to recover, having momentarily forgotten that she'd told Natalie she'd had an appointment to have a filling replaced.

She'd told the little white lie because she'd felt acutely embarrassed by the fact that she'd had to consult a sex therapist, despite how useful the consultation had been, and she was not about to share that information with anyone.

"All right, well, long as you're okay," Natalie said, Josette's edgy demeanor making her skeptical. "I'm headed up to Harlem Hospital to get those supplies they promised us. With traffic being what it is this time of day, it'll most likely be quitting time by the time I'm done getting everything loaded into the van. I guess I'll probably go on home after that and catch up with you in the morning."

"That's fine, Natalie. Have a good one," Josette said, busying her nervous fingers by shuffling some papers on her desk.

Natalie closed the door behind her and Josette relaxed, leaning back in her chair. She wondered when she had become so uptight and repressed about her sexuality. It must have come with motherhood. There were so many expectations about what a mother did and should do, what she was and should be. It was hard to find the balance between natural desires and the images of the quintessential mother. Maybe, without being aware of the change, she had gone too far to the right, becoming overly conservative and repressed. She wondered now if it was too late to find a comfortable place in the middle.

Chapter 7

"Let the church say amen." Pastor Nichols smiled at the congregation, sweat trickling from his furrowed brows.

"Amen."

The congregation responded exuberantly, fired up by the pastor's inspired sermon. Josette looked over at Seth, who appeared to have been moved by the word just delivered as well. He caught her eye, smiled and patted her hand. Josette was so glad that they had taken Natalie and Todd up on their invitation to attend service with them at their church, Holy Baptist, that Sunday. While the Crawfords had been dedicated members of Second Pentecostal Church in Scarsdale for the past ten years, Josette had to admit that she had not heard a service preached like the one she'd just witnessed since she was a little girl back in California. Sometimes a person needed to be reached in a different way. Today, a hand had reached down into the depths of her heart and soul, yanking her back into a spiritual consciousness that made her recognize how fortunate she was to have the life she had. It also forced her to face the fact that she had been blocking her own blessings in many ways. She sat there spent, feeling as though she had truly been washed and renewed. She squeezed her husband's hand and rose to her feet, joining in with the choir as they sang "Worship Him." The timbre of her voice held undeniable clarity as she sang the words, which she believed with conviction.

During the benediction, when Pastor Nichols called for those who believed that Jesus Christ was the one true savior to come forward, Josette and Seth made their way to the front of the church. The good feeling that washed over them carried them forward and they received hugs from the deacons and deaconesses of the church. It was a blessed Sunday.

After the service, Natalie brought the pastor over to meet Josette and Seth. Pastor Nichols was a lot younger than his thunderous voice and dynamic manner of speaking would lead one to believe.

"Mr. and Mrs. Crawford, welcome to God's little house. I'm so glad that you decided to spend this Sunday morning with us," the pastor said, shaking first Seth's hand and then Josette's.

"Thank you, Pastor Nichols. We truly enjoyed the service. You certainly have a way with words," Josette replied.

"Thank you kindly. Might I say that you, Sister Josette, have a beautiful singing voice. I heard you all the way from my place at the pulpit. Fantastic voice. Our choir could certainly use someone like you in it."

"That's what I've been telling Josette myself," Natalie said. "She ought to be singing somewhere...sharing the word."

Josette shot Natalie a look that promised a serious reproach later on.

"Oh, no. I don't really sing in public. This old, scratchy voice of mine is meant for the house only."

"Well, now, I can't say that I would agree with that. I think you're being modest. I'll tell you what. Why don't you think on it some and pray about it. Maybe the Lord might see fit to change your mind, and if he does, come on down to choir practice on Tuesday night at seven o'clock. Trust me, when these folks get to singing and shouting up in here, it is truly something to behold."

Josette blushed, thanking the pastor for his kind words of praise again and promising that she would think about it. On the ride home, she entertained the thought once again, wondering if it was such a bad idea after all. She had promised herself that she would get out and try new things, and maybe this was just another answer to her questions about herself and her life.

By the time they'd made it home, she'd made a decision.

"I think I might go back on Tuesday and check out the choir," she announced to Seth as he pulled the car into their driveway.

"I know," he replied, amused.

"What do you mean? I only just decided. How could you know?"

"Josette, please. I knew from the way your eyes were twinkling back there that you were going to go back. So I guess that means we're switching churches, huh?"

Seth continued laughing at his wife, happy that she was so excited over something that was completely unrelated to the kids, the house or her job at New Hope. He suppressed the bothersome yet recurrent twang of jealousy, which told him that this was yet another thing that would keep Josette away from him. Instead, he tried to view it as an opportunity for her to express herself artistically and for him to get to hear her sweet voice singing every Sunday.

Josette's next session with Dr. Turnup was equally as embarrassing as the first one, especially when the doctor instructed Josette to lie down on a mat on the floor, face up with her arms and legs spread-eagle. She then asked her to close her eyes and picture Seth standing naked above her. After Josette stopped laughing, her cheeks flushed hotly as she realized that Dr. Turnup was serious.

"What?"

"You heard me right, Josette. I want you to use your imagination to visualize your husband standing before you without any clothing on. Come on, close your eyes," the doctor commanded.

Josette followed the doctor's orders, despite her misgivings. Once she had a visual image of Seth, vivid memories came to her of how she'd come to learn his body by exploring every inch of it. From the first time to the hundreds of times thereafter, she'd gotten to know every part of him intimately.

"Now, I'd like you to think about the times you've made love with your husband. How you feel when he's touching you and when you're touching him. How fulfilling those moments are."

The doctor remained silent for a few moments, allowing Josette the time for her mind to roam.

"Josette, think about the way you'd bask in the glow of love, lying in one another's arms afterward. Think about that feeling of connectivity with him—being completely in sync with another human being. How did that make you feel?"

"Full," Josette whispered without hesitation.

"That's a wonderful feeling, isn't it?" Dr. Turn-up asked.

Josette agreed. That was what having a relationship with someone you could depend on felt like. It filled you up physically, mentally, emotionally and sexually. For years she had had that with Seth and lately, she'd begun to believe that they'd lost it. She was realizing now that it was not lost—or at least not so far gone that they could not get it back. She also realized that she couldn't sit back and wait for Seth to do something. It dawned on her that if he was missing her half as much as she was missing him, he may have been waiting for her to do the same.

All day long after that session, Josette had a difficult time concentrating. Every time she sat still for just a moment, one split second was all it took for her mind to return to images of Seth and once that happened, she began to feel a stirring in her belly as if she had an itch on the inside that needed to be scratched. It was getting easier and easier to remember the days when all it took was a look, even a glance from one or the other and it would be on. She and Seth would sneak off, their bodies aflame and their minds racing as they craved one another like a chronic gambler desired a slot machine. She thought that tonight would be the perfect night for them to see if there were any sparks left in the old engine.

She had seen the way Seth's eyes had lit up

when she'd come home with her new hairstyle and her skin glistening the other day after her beauty makeover. But that night wasn't to be the night. Unfortunately, they had had guests. She'd arrived home just moments before Bill and Tracy Keller had rung their doorbell. She'd all but forgotten that it was their turn to host game night. A few years back a group of their neighbors and they had begun a monthly ritual where they gathered at one of their homes for an evening of board games, snacks and drinks. About two years into it, Josette had grown tired of playing board games, and had taught a few of her neighbors how to play Spades. Valerie Andrews had gotten very good at it, but right after she'd proved to be a formidable adversary, making the game much more fun for Josette, she and her husband, Jeremy, had moved to Florida to be closer to her ailing parents.

Fortunately, Seth had remembered that they were having company over that night. He'd made margaritas and had ordered nachos with a warm crab dip and stuffed potato skins from a small Mexican place in town. As he hung up their guests' coats, his eyes remained fixed on Josette. The transformation was amazing and once again he felt like the luckiest man in the world to have been married to a woman for over twenty years and have her look as amazing as the day he'd met her.

Just as they exchanged greetings with the Kellers, both of them going on about how great

Josette looked, the doorbell rang again and in walked Phil Brandt. Phil, who had divorced his second wife, Paris, about four years ago, was apt to show up with a different woman at almost every monthly gathering. This time they were surprised to see that Amber, the twentysomething-year-old Tae Kwon Do instructor, was still hanging in there.

The other regular participants in game night were the Woodrow couple, but Albert Woodrow had suffered a stroke a few weeks back and his recovery was very slow going. His wife, Miki, had been running herself ragged between taking care of him and overseeing the furniture gallery they ran in town. Every Sunday since Albert's stroke, Josette had made a large dinner for them to help alleviate some of the pressure Miki was experiencing. Similarly others in the neighborhood had their children drag the trash cans out from the side of the Woodrow residence to the curb on trash day and rake leaves every few days from the front lawn. In addition, Phil had been mowing their lawn along with his every week. That was the type of neighborhood in which they lived. That was what had kept Seth and Josette there for all the years they'd lived there.

The night was filled with laughter and good-natured fun. Seth's arm lingered around Josette's shoulder for much of the night and she loved the feeling of it there. The twinkle in his eyes told her that he was feeling the same way as she was, and both of them held the expectation of what was to come. Unfortunately, by the time the guests left, Seth, who had never been much of a drinker, was three sheets to the wind and could barely climb the stairs to their bedroom. Josette helped him into bed, where he passed out immediately and, feeling no pain herself, she was asleep almost as fast as he was. The closeness they had shared that night as they'd hung with friends was a step in the right direction and that night, her dreams left her feeling full again.

Chapter 8

Three weeks of Mama Sa's rhythmic workout, three times each week, had Josette feeling as limber as a wet noodle. There was a tightness around her midsection and a firmness in her thighs and calves that had not been there before. Tonight she had gone it alone, as Natalie had been feeling under the weather. Josette was tempted to skip the class herself, but she knew that doing so might cause her muscles to soften up on her again. She liked the way she was beginning to look and to feel, and she did not want to stop the progress.

She arrived moments before class was scheduled to begin, sweaty and out of breath from having to rush from work. It had been a grueling day, most of it spent on the telephone trying to secure services for clients that the red tape of the bureaucratic system said they were ineligible to receive but which they desperately needed. Once she shut her office door, however, she was determined to leave those troubles there until tomorrow.

She slipped in one of the back lines, scarcely having time to look around before Mama Sa began calling out the warm-up. She did notice, however, that standing beside her and moving with the agility of Frankenstein was a tall, muscular, brown-skinned man—the only man in the classroom besides the drummers. She kept her eyes averted, attempting to suppress her surprise. Not once in the three weeks she had been taking the class had she seen a man present, counting out the drummers and the husbands who congregated in the lobby waiting for their ladies. She was unsure of what to make of this gentleman in his navy-blue sweatpants and tank top, as he huffed and puffed, trying in desperation to keep up with the fast tempos and intricate steps. He had two left feet and he was unable to get either one of them to move in the right direction at the right moment. He crashed into Josette more than once, each time smiling apologetically.

Josette discreetly took a few steps away, moving forward of their line so as to avoid colliding with the uncoordinated newcomer. Soon thereafter, she was able to push aside all distracting thoughts and became engrossed in the way the drumbeat and the motions made her body feel. By the time class had ended, Josette, covered in sweat and feeling as if she could dance for another hour, had all but forgotten about anything else.

"Excuse me…could you tell me where I could get a pair of those," he said.

Josette spun around to find the tall, rhythymless newcomer standing behind her.

"Excuse me?" she replied.

"Those," he said, pointing to the tan half-sole shoes she wore on her otherwise bare feet.

Josette looked down at her toes, relieved that her pedicure was still fresh on what she believed to be one of her nicest features, her feet. She glanced over at his Diesel sneaker-clad feet.

"Oh, I'm sorry. I wasn't sure what you were talking about. These are called Sandasols and they basically protect the balls of your feet when dancing. They're better on your feet than dancing barefoot and they help to prevent calluses from forming. My friend Natalie picked them up for me from a little dance-wear shop down on Broadway, near Park Row."

"Broadway? Whereabouts?"

"It's on one of those side streets down there that are named after people. Like Charles or Ann Street. Something like that. Uh… Let's see… How can I direct you…? Do you know where that big Starbucks is?"

"Oh, okay. I think I know the area a little. Maybe I'll head over there for a pair and walk around until I find it. I'm sure someone will be able to direct me."

"So, you're planning to continue taking Mama Sa's class?" Josette asked.

She hoped she didn't sound judgmental of him, but she couldn't help herself. It seemed out of the norm to see a man of her age taking an African dance class. For a fleeting moment, she wondered if he was gay. She reconsidered that last thought because most of the gay men she'd ever known were excellent dancers and that was certainly not a way she would categorize him.

"Yes, I am. I loved it. Why, is that strange?" he asked.

Josette's face flushed from embarrassment.

"No...no, I didn't mean ..." she stammered. "I didn't mean anything by that. It's just ...well, you *are* the only man in the class," she finished, lowering her eyes from his bemused face.

"I see. Well, I hope no one is offended by my presence. A good friend of mine told me about the class and I thought it would be a great way to lose some of these midlife pounds I've packed on." He smiled.

"You look like you're in pretty good shape to me," Josette complimented.

She was immediately embarrassed again. She hoped that the man didn't take her compliment as anything more than a friendly remark. She clumsily wiped the perspiration from her neck and face again. Stuffing her towel into her gym bag, she was acutely aware of his presence as he stood silently watching her. After she dropped the bag for the second time, he stooped to help her, retrieving it from the floor and handing it to her.

"Thank you," she whispered.

"You're quite welcome…and thank you…for the compliment."

There was a moment of comfortable silence between them as Josette looked up into warm eyes. After only a few moments of dialogue, Josette was certain about two things. The first was that this man was definitely not gay, and secondly, she was feeling sensations that told her it was definitely time for her to go home to her husband.

"Clinton Parks," he said, extending his hand. "Everyone except my mama calls me Clint, however."

"Josette Crawford," she said, smiling, shaking his outstretched hand.

"It's been a pleasure to meet you," Clint said.

He followed Josette out of the classroom and into the corridor. As they stopped to retrieve their coats from the coatroom, Clint reached out and helped Josette into her jacket.

"Thank you," she said over her shoulder.

Josette hurried out of the studio, without giving

Mr. Parks another look or word. Unbeknownst to her, he watched her walk away, tempted to pursue.

"I'm telling you, Natalie, the man is not gay, very attractive and says that he definitely plans on continuing with the class," Josette said.

She held the cordless phone tucked beneath her chin as she spread honey-mustard glaze over the roasted pork she'd made for dinner. She had been home for little under an hour and had called with the intention of checking on Natalie. Once she'd gotten to talking, however, Clinton Parks's name had tumbled from her lips, as he had been tumbling around her mind since she'd met him earlier that evening.

"Well," said Natalie through a stuffed nose, her voice raspy, "I'm sure he won't last. I've seen Mama Sa go really hard on the men and sooner or later, they all quit. Men think that because they're strong and can toss around a football, dance is a piece of cake. She'll fix his wagon."

"I don't know, Natalie. I mean, he was a little stiff, but he seemed like a fast learner. After a while he started to keep up a little bit. I don't think he did too badly considering this was his first class."

"Mmm, sounds like you're his personal little cheerleader," Natalie remarked.

"Ha-ha. I was just saying that if a man is *man* enough to take an African dance class full of women, he deserves a shot at it," Josette defended.

"Whatever. I guess time will tell if he can hang. Personally, I doubt it, but I'll have to see this with my own eyes. Aah-choo!" Natalie exploded.

"You sound terrible. I hope you're planning to keep your germs at home tomorrow," Josette said.

"Gee, thanks for the concern, Josette," Natalie said, laughing at first and then falling into a fit of chest-raking coughs. "What are you and Seth up to this evening?" she asked once she recovered her breath.

"Nothing much. He's working a little bit late. I've made dinner. Same ole, same ole," Josette said.

"Josette, can I say something to you? I mean, feel free to tell me to mind my business, but just hear me out."

"Sure, what's up?"

"Well, the other day…I was looking for some sanitary napkins, you know, in your bottom desk drawer where you usually keep them, and well, I found that book you're reading…the one by Dr. Turnup," Natalie said hesitantly.

"I see," Josette said, her face growing hot.

"Look, I wasn't prying or snooping or anything. But anyway, I saw the book and I just want you to know that I think it's great that you're getting in touch with your sexuality. There's nothing wrong with, you know, getting answers."

"I know," Josette finally managed to say.

"Good. That's all that I wanted to say," Natalie said.

"Natalie." Josette sighed. "I can't believe that at forty-six years old, I'm reading a book to find out how to make love to my husband."

There, she'd finally said to someone what had been plaguing her thoughts for the past few weeks. Someone besides Dr. Turnup, who, despite how comforting she was, was still a doctor, and Bernardo, who was a man—very insightful, but still a man.

"Josette, what's so wrong with that? You and Seth have been together for a zillion years. Shoot, that in and of itself is a miracle in this day and age. So what, you've got to brush up on your skills a little bit. At least you're still interested in each other. My parents have been married for almost forty years and I swear if they say two words to one another every day, that's a lot."

"I don't know, Natalie. I just love him so much and it occurred to me the other day that, well, if I'm not making him happy, you know, in that way… I'm sure there are women waiting to do the honors, if you know what I mean," Josette said.

"Josette, I've seen the way Seth looks at you. You've got to know that that man adores you and you him, right?"

"Yeah. I'm just worried about us. With the kids practically grown and out of the house, it's just us. What do we do?"

"For starters, tonight, Josette, why don't you pretend that it's just you and Seth in this whole big world. Pretend it's your one-year wedding anniversary. What would you do?"

Josette didn't need much more inspiration than that. All the thoughts that had been running around in her head seemed to come to one dramatic conclusion. She wanted her man. She placed dinner in the oven, cleaned up the mess in the kitchen and headed upstairs. She took a quick, hot shower, scrubbing and exfoliating her skin until it felt smooth and squeaky-clean. The products she'd purchased from Gabrielle Edwards were doing wonders on her. She loosened the ponytail holder she'd placed at the back of her head during dance class and washed her hair with strawberry-scented shampoo. She ran a blow dryer through her hair, leaving it slightly damp to air-dry the rest of the way.

She lathered perfumed lotion all over her body, from her neck down to her toes. For the third time that day she brushed her teeth, flossed and rinsed, then cleansed her face and moisturized. She applied a pale pink lip gloss and mauve eye shadow. She searched through her top dresser drawer, removing the linen bag she kept, untouched, in the back. Inside she found several negligees and teddies, items she hadn't worn in several years. She tried on a few of them and, despite the few pounds she had lost in the past few weeks, it was difficult to find one that fit properly. Finally, she struck gold with a black lace teddy Seth had bought her for Valentine's Day about four or five years back. It fit her like a glove, boosting her bosom and giving the appearance of flattening her tummy. She stood looking in the full-length mirror on the back of her bedroom door. The same mirror that had shattered her self-image just a few weeks ago now flattered her. She combed out her hair, brushed it until it shone, and donned a bathrobe, heading downstairs to finish out her plans for seduction.

Chapter 9

Seth pulled into the driveway, turned the car's ignition off, but sat for a while, unwilling to go inside the house just now. It was early November, and both of the kids were firmly engrossed in their college lives. His hopes for what that would mean for his marriage had been dashed. While Josette was no longer melancholy over the empty house, she was not paying Seth any more attention than she had before. In fact, she was home less and less as the weeks went by. First it was that dance class that she was taking three evenings a week, followed by dinner with her friends. Now that she was singing in the choir at Natalie's church, she went to practice one evening out of the week, for three hours at a time. Saturdays, she was always out on errands, shopping or something. He barely saw her and when he did, she seemed different to him. On the rare evenings that they sat down to dinner together, she was chatty and bubbly. She talked about the great things going on at New Hope and was very excited over some federal grant money they had been able to secure. She listened intently to his talk about his cases and the office. On the surface, it appeared that things between them were fantastic. But a closer examination of their relationship revealed a committed friendship, solid and enduring. The only problem was that that was all there seemed to be.

Seth knew that he should have seized the opportunities to get closer to his wife. For the life of him, he didn't understand why he couldn't just talk to her about the way he was feeling. Here he was, a man of prestige and power, a man whose very livelihood depended on his skills as an orator and his ability to present a convincing case. Lately, he was more unsure of himself with Josette than he had been as a pimply faced fourteen-year-old with his first crush. He was reluctant to make a move on her because he was unsure of how she would react. He was not a man who handled rejection well, no matter how congenial he appeared to be.

Maybe their love life had run its course. Seth hated to even think about that prospect but it kept finding its way into his thought process. Or, it could be that she no longer found him attractive. He knew that it was not the other way around because he was just as turned on by her as he had been the first time he'd laid eyes on her. Sure, things had changed. They had both aged. He knew that he was no longer the stud of his youth, but none of that registered when he looked at his wife or recollected the way she'd opened herself up to him completely on their wedding night two decades ago. He had been her first mature love and he had wanted to please her immensely. He'd intended not only to be her first, but her only forever, and he never wanted her to wonder what lovemaking with another man would be like. All along he had thought that he'd been satisfying her. At least that was what she used to tell him.

Tonight, rejection or not, he intended to tell his wife how he felt. Tonight, he wanted to do more than hold her in his arms and give and get the customary friendly peck on the cheek. She was his life and right now, he felt as though a part of him were no longer among the living. Tonight he wanted to hear her moan his name, the way she used to in a sweet, passion-filled voice. Tonight, he didn't want dinner, conversation or anything else. Tonight he wanted to feel the fullness of her hips in his hands as she straddled him and hear her cry out as he hit her spot. He took a deep breath, opened the car door and climbed out. His heart raced and his palms grew sweaty despite the cool breeze, yet he forged ahead.

When Seth entered the house, he was acutely aware that something was amiss. All of the lights were off. Was she not at home? That thought filled him with crushing disappointment. Now that he had finally worked up the nerve to reach out to his wife, could she really have gone out somewhere? He remembered that her car had been in the garage when he'd pulled up the driveway and was almost filled with relief until his mind told him that she could have been picked up by a friend or chosen to take a taxi.

He moved through the house, his emotions warring within him, searching for the unwanted handwritten note from Josette that would crush his plans. The kitchen was empty. There wasn't even a plate of food on the stove waiting for him, something she normally did if she was going to be out when he came in. He peered into the dark, formal dining room off the rear of the kitchen. Nothing. He retraced his steps through the kitchen and returned to the foyer. He continued down the hallway and stopped before the living-room doors, which were shut. He leaned his ear closer to the crack between the doors and heard a trumpet playing softly. Confusion knotted his brow as he turned the knob and stepped inside.

The sight took his breath away. In all of his forty-seven years he could honestly say that

nothing had ever shocked or surprised him. In a
world full of equal measures of calm and calamity,
he had never been confronted with anything far
removed from his expectations. Tonight, however,
was a whole different story. The room was bathed
in candlelight, issuing from candles placed all
around the room. The unmistakable instrumental
serenade of Seth's favorite jazz trumpeter, Wynton
Marsalis, flowed from the speakers mounted on
the walls in the far corners of the room. A small
table set for two and laden with covered dishes and
champagne waited on the left-hand side of the
room, where his recliner used to sit. The thing that
shocked him, literally drawing the air from his
body like a punch to the gut, was Josette. On their
bear-skin rug, in front of a glowing fire in the fireplace, sat Josette. Her gorgeous hair hung down her
head, framing her beautiful face. He'd told her that
her new hairstyle was nice, but even then he'd
known that was an understatement. He'd wanted to
get tangled up in it, bury his face in it and never
come out. Tonight she wore a black lace teddy,
which hugged her breasts in an inviting manner. He
remembered buying that teddy a while back and
then never before getting the chance to see her in
it. Her bare legs, always shapely in his opinion,
were looking toned and tight, and he could already
imagine them wrapped around his neck, her inner
thighs squeezing his face. She held a champagne
flute in her hands.

"Welcome home, baby," she said softly.

Seth dropped his briefcase, taking a tentative step into the room. He was mesmerized by her and it wasn't until she commanded him closer with a wiggle of her finger that he was able to move from the position he seemed to be rooted in. He walked across the room and sank down to his knees on the rug next to her. She lifted her glass to his lips and he drank greedily, the liquid sizzling in his burning throat.

"Josette," he managed to say.

"Shh," she said, setting the glass down and placing her finger on his lips to silence him.

She rose up onto her knees and began unbuttoning his shirt. Her fingers trembled, a sign of the nervousness and desire she felt. It took her several tries to completely open and remove his shirt. She then leaned forward and, when her lips first touched his, his world seemed to come together. For the first time in months, her tongue teased his mouth, sliding into the opening of his parted lips, and that action alone was strong enough to put his pieces back together again.

He inhaled deeply, the scent of her womanness caressing his nostrils and his senses. She kissed him deeply and he returned her fervor. His hands found their way into her hair. He couldn't remember the last time he'd been allowed to explore the glorious mane on her head. He tangled his hands in the softness as she licked and sucked at his lips and tongue. The sounds he began to hear were his own moans, as he was unable to deny the pleasure she was giving him. He slid his hands up and down her silky arms, slowly moving to the lace teddy that so intrigued him. He hadn't seen his wife in something this sexy in a long time, more years than he could count. He explored her, the round fullness of her body. She was all woman— soft and sensual.

For her part, Josette was happy that she had managed to lose five pounds since she had been taking dance classes, but still felt slightly uncomfortable wearing something so revealing and minuscule. She knew that she was not the same curvaceous woman that Seth had married and hoped that he still found her body appealing.

She noticed him looking at her attire, his eyes aflame.

"Do I look okay?" she asked timidly.

Seth struggled to find his voice. He ran two fingers across the lace that restrained her left breast.

"You are so beautiful, Josette," he finally managed to whisper.

"Really?" she asked.

To Seth, she sounded like the young woman he'd first married. She was so unsure of herself back then and now, but wanting to please him and be pleasing to him in every way.

"Oh, Josette, my pretty, pretty Josette. Woman, don't you know that you are the most beautiful woman in the world?"

"Stop it, Seth," she said, placing her hand on top of his, still lingering on her breast.

"No, I won't. You are magnificent," he breathed.

He leaned forward, his lips replacing his hand on the flesh of her breast. He kissed each one, slowly sliding the straps of her teddy from her shoulders. Her back arched and she threw her head back as his lips made contact with her neck. He freed her breasts and stared down at the large, fleshy mounds, their sienna-brown nipples erect and pointing at him. He kissed each one, filling his hands and mouth with them. Josette's breath caught in her throat and then issued from her in short bursts of delight.

This was the stuff dreams were made of—at least Seth's dreams. He had so many thoughts of what he wanted to do to Josette that he couldn't think straight as the thoughts collided in his brain. Finally, he stopped thinking and allowed himself to be carried away by the sheer joy of touching her again. He remembered the first time she had taken him in her mouth. It was something that she had never imagined herself doing, but that was the thing about passion. Once it consumed you, there were not very many limits that remained unbreakable. He had not urged her to do it, although it was something they had discussed in the past. From time to time over the course of their marriage, she'd indulge and, like everything else Josette did, she was perfect at it. Tonight was one of those nights.

He was her love prisoner, and she used and abused his body so deliciously that he thought for sure he'd lose his mind. Her mouth teased him to attention, turning his manhood into an engorged, loaded gun.

Their naked bodies were scorching with the heat of desire and they touched one another as if they had been lost at the North Pole wearing nothing but their birthday suits for the past twenty-four hours. Now, they sought heat—lavalike and fiery. When Josette released his erection, Seth ran his hands up and down the length of her body. He was amazed at how soft her skin was—softer than he remembered it being. He returned his attention to her perfect breasts, still captivated by the fullness of them and the way the large nipples pointed at him, daring him to suckle them. He wanted to taste every inch of her and attempted to do so, but Josette stopped him. She was running this show tonight and he was relegated to being her willing slave. She climbed on top of him, moving her lower body in a circular motion that teased him to the point of insanity.

When she finally allowed him to enter her waiting nest, he felt as if he had been on a long, grueling trip and had finally returned home. Her wide hips and fleshy behind filled his hands as he held on to her for dear life. She moved in slow, deliberate movements, taking him closer and closer to reaching the clouds above the earth. Finally, almost as if she were giving him permission, she brought him over the summit. His orgasm was earth-shattering and he swore that if he lived to be a hundred there would never be a night to rival this one.

"Damn, baby. That was amazing," Seth said when she finally released him and collapsed beside him. He lay spent and covered in perspiration—his own and hers.

"Mmm, hmm," Josette agreed.

She snuggled closer to Seth's chest as he drew his arm tightly around her body. He pulled the throw blanket from the sofa to shield their nakedness from the chill, although he'd much rather look at her bare body, glistening with their water.

"Josette, I could come home to a welcome like this every night, but I've got to ask you something," Seth said.

"What's that?"

"What's going on? I mean, what's gotten into you lately?"

"What do you mean, Seth?" Josette laughed.

"You're taking dance classes, you're singing in the choir…hanging out, shopping. If I didn't know any better, I'd swear you're going through some sort of female midlife crisis or something," Seth replied.

"Midlife crisis? Well, for your information, Mr. Crawford, I'm nowhere near being close to having a midlife crisis, because I've got years to go before I reach the middle of my life," Josette said.

She rolled on top of Seth, kissing her husband's smiling lips as his body responded to the smoothness of her skin.

"So to what can I attribute this wonderful welcome I received tonight?" he asked.

"Why don't you just chalk it up to the fact that I love you, Seth Crawford. I love you more than life itself, and I just want to make sure you know that and that you never forget it," Josette said, tears swimming in her eyes.

Seth kissed each eyelid, feeling close to tears of his own. He didn't know what he'd done to deserve this minor miracle, but he was glad that he'd received it. One night of pleasure with his wife was worth a lifetime of trials and tribulations. It might have been the power of positive thinking or divine intervention—it didn't matter. Whatever the case, he was determined to make sure that the rest of their lives were filled with nights like this one.

He moved beneath her, slowly pressing himself against her as their tongues explored one another's mouths deeply. She responded, her hips gyrating in the most sensual dance he'd ever felt. It was going to be a long night.

Chapter 10

Like a man possessed, Seth floated through the next few days. His behavior was like an adolescent who'd just discovered the wonders of sexual intercourse with someone other than himself. He felt like a young man again and every time he looked at his wife, whether she was brushing her teeth in the bathroom or adding fabric softener to the rinse cycle, to him she was the same blushing bride he'd exchanged vows with in a tiny little church in Sacramento, California.

Seated at a bar one night, having drinks with his cousin Louis, Seth was completely distracted. He was having a difficult time listening to Louis lament over his soon-to-be ex-wife, who had left him for a younger man. Their divorce would be final in just a few more weeks and Louis's world had all but come to an end. Seth tried to comfort his cousin, wanting to be a shoulder for him to lean on. However, all Seth could think about was the fact that Josette was waiting at home for him.

"Louis, man, I think the best thing for you to do right now is to concentrate on work. Man, I'm telling you, nothing clears the brain like a hard day of work. Haven't you been talking about expanding your practice for the past few years?"

"Yeah, so?" Louis said, tipping his second glass of bourbon up to his lips and taking a long, hard swallow.

"So what's been holding you back?"

Louis didn't respond. He just sat staring blankly at Seth. A few years Seth's junior, Louis had been the closest thing to a brother that Seth had had. Coming up, Louis had always been a bit of a ladies' man, taking after his father it seemed. Louis Crawford Sr. had never married his son's mother, nor had he married the mothers of his three daughters. He didn't believe in marriage and he had never been the type of man who put down roots. He was the proverbial rolling stone and, while he had not been around long enough at any given time to teach his son anything, he had managed to impart his "hit it and quit it" philosophy on him. Seth had always cautioned his cousin Louis that his player ways would eventually catch up with him and they had—in the form of Hurricane Serena. Louis had fallen hard for Serena, a Southern beauty with down-home charm but big-city dreams. He'd given up all of his women almost instantaneously, becoming a one-woman man. Within six months of dating, he'd proposed to her, despite all of the warning signs and all of the words of caution from family and friends, including Seth.

"For at least five of the seven years that you and Serena were married, you were running behind her, checking up on her and following her around."

"Hey—"

"No, don't *hey* me. It's the truth and you know it," Seth said, losing patience with his cousin. "Look, man, I don't mean to disrespect you, but it's time for you to face facts."

Seth clasped the glass that Louis was lifting to his lips. Louis looked at Seth, considering his serious expression for a moment before returning the glass to the table.

"I'm listening," he said.

"I don't want to say that Serena's not a good woman. Maybe in some ways, on a level that we just never got to see, she is. All I know is that she was not a good woman for you. You practically drove yourself crazy behind that woman."

"I love her," Louis said.

Seth shook his head, disgusted by how pathetic his cousin sounded.

"Okay, and at the end of the day, where'd all that love leave you? She left you for a washed-up basketball player, who wasn't even that good when he was in his prime. I mean, come on, Louis, how can you be this distraught over someone like that? Serena just about drove you crazy and now that she's gone, I say good riddance."

Louis began to nod his head slowly, seeming to be emboldened by Seth's words.

"You're right. You are right," Louis said.

"There you go. That's the spirit. Just keep thinking about how good your life is going to be now that you're free. You can work on your business without the distractions she was causing you. With your knowledge and expertise, you could triple your customer base. All you need to do is to redirect some of that energy toward you and stop thinking about Serena."

Louis seemed to be on the right track and, while Seth was glad to see that his cousin had been talked back from the edge of depression, he was equally pleased by the prospect that soon he'd be able to take his leave of him without a guilty conscience. For as disturbed as he was by his cousin's woes, he was fighting the hard-on of his life as visions of Josette danced around in his brain.

When two young women invited themselves over to their table, Seth knew that it was time to go. For his part, he had absolutely no interest in the women because in comparison to what he had waiting for him at home, they weren't even a close second. He realized, however, that Louis was way too vulnerable to ward off the advances of anything in a skirt and heels. With insincere apologies, he paid their tab and ushered Louis out of the bar and into a yellow cab. He would have driven him home himself, but he'd already been delayed and enough was enough.

True to his word, Seth pulled out all the stops to make sure that his and Josette's renewed passion had a place to prosper. He sent flowers to Josette at her office, took her out to her favorite bistro for dinner and made sure that he was home from the office by six o'clock every night. When they stayed in, he ordered takeout or cooked one of his few but signature dishes, so that her time in the kitchen was nonexistent. He even bought her a negligee— red and minimal, which he enjoyed taking off her as much as he enjoyed seeing her in. There were times when Josette would blush and grow uncomfortable at his expressions of adoration and utter worship. She still sometimes fell victim to feelings of self-consciousness about her body, something that was foreign to him, but nonetheless, a valid feeling brought on by the changes of life that motherhood and aging brought. He assured her, with his words and actions, that she was more beautiful to him than she had ever been.

Josette slowly began to reconnect with the sexual and sensual side of herself that had grown dormant over the years. With Seth's enduring passion and in-surmountable libido, in addition to weekly discussions and tips from Dr. Turnup, she began to be less concerned about what once was and focused more on the present. She and Seth began to explore sexual positions and toys, which she'd shyly introduced after discovering them in literature. Seth was particularly fond of the heated massage oil she'd brought home one day, which smelled of mint and eucalyptus. After ordering him to remove all of his clothing and lie prostrate on their bed, Josette had poured some out into the palm of her hands, rubbing them together for about twenty seconds. She'd gently taken his member into her hot hands and had begun rubbing the oil up and down the length of him. Within a few seconds he'd grown erect, and continued to grow harder still the longer she'd rubbed him. He'd been filled with a mind-blowing intensity as he'd watched her handle his throbbing instrument and finally, when she'd straddled him, sliding down onto him expertly, he'd felt as if he would come unglued. The sultry, rhythmic movement of her hips on top of him had been intoxicating. She'd kept him on the brink of climaxing for the better part of an hour, deliciously teasing him until he'd been exhausted. When he finally had climaxed, it had felt as if every ounce of fluid had been sucked from his body. Moments later, Josette had exploded herself before collapsing on top of his still-tingling body.

This was just one of the many positions that

they'd rediscovered as they rekindled the animalistic fervor that they'd shared in their youth. Josette had surprised him one day when she'd stopped their lovemaking, got down on the floor on all fours and had enticed him to enter her from behind. This was a position she had previously adamantly disapproved of and, consequently, he had never attempted to partake of her in this fashion. She had always cited physical discomfort as well as a mental repulsion at the idea of it.

"Are you sure?" he'd asked now, panting with passion.

Josette's answer had been to reach back and guide Seth into her waiting, welcome center. The pleasure she'd received was startling, and her satisfied moans had aroused him tenfold.

More than just sexual gratification had been awakened in Seth and Josette. The friendship that had developed between them over the years seemed to come full circle. There was an eagerness to talk to one another that had dulled over the years, as the tendency to take one's mate for granted had become a natural pattern.

Personally, Josette was fulfilled in her own life as it related to a new discovery of the self and not to what she was doing for other people. She continued taking dance lessons and singing with the choir, activities that provided a spiritual stimulation that awakened an utterly personal part of her soul. She still missed her children, especially Marcus, who had yet to come home for a visit. However, the loneliness she had expected to bombard her was kept at bay as she read more, loved more and simply enjoyed getting to know herself again. One Saturday morning as she sat straightening out some things they had stored in the attic, she came across a journal of poetry that she had begun when the children had been in elementary school. Initially, it had been born out of boredom, but soon she'd found that writing in that journal allowed her to tap into her own thoughts and feelings uncensored. After reading through pages that she had written over a decade ago, laughing at times and crying at others, she began writing in the journal again. With the freedom of a recently exonerated death-row inmate, she used her pen to explore her soul.

Chapter 11

As the couple cuddled like newlyweds late one evening watching the news, a commercial came on that caught both of their attentions. At precisely the same moment, as visions of crystal-blue water stretching for as many miles as the eye could see and beyond flashed before their eyes, Seth and Josette were lulled into the idea of taking a spur-of-the-moment vacation. They had talked about going to Hawaii for their twenty-first anniversary, which was approaching in June, but decided as they lay watching an advertisement for a cruise line that they could not wait that long. Seven days and seven nights away from work, with nothing to do but lie in each other's arms, was way too appealing. The fact that the idea had come to them both at the same time served to seal its perfection.

The next morning, Seth logged on to his computer at the office and within half an hour had booked their trip. He called Josette at her office and listened with pride as she gushed over it and over him. With the phone cradled beneath her neck, she bragged to her coworkers how spontaneous and romantic her husband was, and he puffed out his chest like a proud peacock. They spent the next few days making arrangements to cover their respective business obligations, as well as making sure the kids had enough money in their bank accounts to tide them over. After leaving contact information with various people along with strict admonitions not to contact them, they headed off to what proved to be the best medicine for their marriage they could have taken. This was the first trip outside of long weekends that they had taken alone since the kids had been born, and they were filled with a sort of guilty pleasure at doing it.

They flew out to Los Angeles, California, and boarded a luxury cruise ship, on which they sailed for seven glorious days up and down the Mexican Riviera. In contrast to prior vacations, they did not do much sightseeing this time as their only interests lay in each other. They lay around on deck, reading from the same novel or just relaxing and enjoying the mild weather. It was wonderful to take a break from the harsh November weather they'd left behind as autumn reluctantly gave way to winter in New York City. They sipped fruity elixirs out of ridiculous cups with fruit sticking out of them. They ate too much, unconcerned with calorie counting. They visited the gym together, mostly just to enjoy the sauna or the spa services. Occasionally, they rode the bicycles or walked on the treadmill, but neither one worked out enough to break a sweat. Their favorite pastime, however, was a private, one-on-one recreation that did not require them to leave the minisuite stateroom in which Seth had booked them. They made love as if they had never done so before—sometimes it was slow and ardent, like new lovers discovering one another for the first time. Sometimes, when passion overtook their senses, they became acrobats and body contortionists, seeking to take one another to new heights of pleasure.

Seth was unaware that Josette had become quite the student of lovemaking and sexual exploration. Through her sessions with Dr. Turnup and the literature she had been reading, she'd come to develop a further appreciation for lovemaking as an art. She learned the importance of listening to the body's senses and relying on instinct and desire to set the tone of lovemaking as opposed to being ruled by the fevered brain, which was in no way capable of thinking clearly once it was sexually aroused. Before now, Josette had been a one-climax type of woman. Once she'd reached her moment of satisfaction, she'd been completely spent and unable to engage any further for a while. Now, she was not only able to regulate when she came, but how often as well. She would climax and, although it was obvious to Seth when she did, she would continue to work his body almost without skipping a beat. He had heard that after forty women really came into their own sexually and he could now testify to that fact himself. He couldn't believe that some men his age preferred young women—who could possibly desire a twenty-year-old when he had all of this? Certainly not him.

What Seth enjoyed most was having his wife all to himself. Having her undivided attention did more for his spirit than anything else could have. They talked about things they hadn't had time to even think about in years. They reminisced on how far they had come in their lives and for him, it was magical. Josette began to feel like that pretty young girl who'd been so enamored by the handsome pre-law student who'd pursued her all those years ago. Slowly, she began to shed her inhibitions and her fears about aging and realized that the woman she had become was just another layer of the one Seth had fallen in love with. At his insistence, she walked around their stateroom nude, not feeling ashamed of the brushstrokes time had painted, and her skin burned under his lustful gaze. Sharing her

heart, her mind and her body with Seth in this un-
interrupted haven was like food to her soul and she
ate greedily.

They absolutely lost themselves on the island of
Catalina, third largest of the Channel Islands, both
literally and figuratively. The island's natural
beauty spread over fifty miles of shoreline, and
included secluded coves and dramatic views,
which were intoxicating to them. Seth and Josette
soon learned why the destination had earned a reputation as *the island of romance.* They found a
private spot on the secluded cove called Little
Harbor, which was located on the southwest shore,
and after becoming drunk off of a combination of
the sun, the island's popular drink called Buffalo
Milk and each other, they fell asleep. When they
awoke, the sun had begun to set and they were
alone. It was almost six-thirty and their ship was
set to sail at seven o'clock. Panicked, they raced
back to the main gate, where a sleepy security
guard informed them that there was no way they'd
make it back on time. He explained that there was
a ten-year waiting list for the right to own a car on
the island, and consequently, there were not very
many vehicles available. Fortunately, a local fish-
erman overheard their tale and ushered them into
the back of his golf cart, the preferred mode of
transportation, and breaking every speed and safety
limit in place, he got them to the port at Green
Pleasure Pier in the center of downtown Avalon,

where they were to catch a tender boat out to the ship within fifteen minutes. Unfortunately, the final tender boat had already left.

At this point, the couple was about ready to give up, leave their belongings on the ship, spend the night there and find a way home the next day. After giving the matter a second thought, however, they realized that without identification, which they'd left in the safe in their cabin, this might prove to be a difficult task. Lady luck shone on them again when a tender-boat operator returned from his break and solved their crisis. He telephoned the ship and informed the personnel that he had two late passengers. He was granted permission to carry them out to the ship. By the time they made it back onboard, embarrassed and exhausted, all they could do was laugh at themselves. For the remainder of their cruise they didn't venture off the ship for more than an hour at a time, which was fine with them because they much preferred their indoor activities, anyway.

By the time they returned home, all they could do was giggle with embarrassment when they realized that they'd only managed to take about five photographs with the digital camera they'd brought along. When friends and family inquired about the ports of call, they had a hard time remembering one from the other—with the exception of Catalina, of course. They'd bought a couple of souvenirs from the ports of Cabo San Lucas and Ensenada, but everything else had been purchased on the ship the night before they'd been scheduled to return home. Yet when asked if they had a good time, the breathless *yes* that issued collectively from their lips said it all.

Chapter 12

"That's not the least bit funny, Dr. Tucker," Josette said.

She hopped off the examining table hurriedly and plucked her blouse off of the chair where she had laid it. She had a million things to do that day and she certainly did not have time to be the butt of an old man's attempts to relieve his personal boredom by using her as comic relief.

"Uh, Josette, I'm not joking," Dr. Tucker replied, holding a printout of Josette's test results in his hand.

Josette froze, keeping her back turned to the doctor. Slowly she turned around to see his unsmiling face. Dr. Tucker was in his midsixties. He was a soft-spoken, brown-skinned man with brown eyes and a short afro of soft gray hair. Dr. Tucker had been Josette's gynecologist and obstetrician for the past twenty years. He had delivered both of her children, held her hand through two cancer scares and had been as much of a friend to her as he was her doctor. It would be a shame to have to stop coming to him because obvious senility had descended upon the poor man.

"Dr. Tucker, I assure you…I cannot possibly be pregnant," Josette with as much certainty as she knew her name to be Josette Marie Crawford.

"And why can't you be?" Dr. Tucker asked with amusement.

He had delivered this news to countless women over the years and more often than not, they were not prepared to hear it. That was especially true in the case of older women such as Josette. He handed the printed sheet of paper to Josette, who accepted it hesitantly as if it were contagious.

"Because…well, you know I've started the change. And remember, the chemotherapy?" Josette said reluctantly.

She hated to even mention the word *chemotherapy* because that period, six years ago, had been the scariest time of her entire life. A routine Pap smear had led to the discovery of ovarian cancer shortly after her fortieth birthday. Josette remembered the day she'd received the phone call

from Dr. Tucker's assistant, saying the doctor
wanted her to come in to discuss the results of her
latest tests as if it had been this morning. It had
been before she had taken the position at New
Hope. She'd dropped the kids off at school—
Marcus had been in the seventh grade and Simone,
the eighth. Neither had wanted to take the school
bus any longer, like some of the other kids in their
neighborhood did, because apparently, it was no
longer cool to ride the cheese bus, as they'd called
it. Josette then stopped to pick up Seth's shirts from
the dry cleaner's and grabbed a couple of cases of
Lady's special dog food from the veterinarian's
office. She'd had a taste for lamb all week long so
she then went by the butcher shop, where Niko, the
elderly Italian man who owned the store, selected
his best cut of meat for her, his favorite customer.
After chatting with Niko for a while, Josette got
into her car and headed home. Her cell phone rang
as she turned onto her block. When the receptionist spoke those words, she immediately knew that
something was wrong. When the doctor got on the
line at her request but refused to go into details over
the telephone, she promised to come into the office
within the hour. When they'd moved out to Larchmont, Josette had considered changing to a local
doctor, but had never done so. She was comfortable
with Dr. Tucker, loved his staff and his offices. At
that point, however, she wished for the first time
that she had switched to a local physician because

she really didn't know if she'd be able to stand the wait as she traveled into Manhattan. Sitting in her driveway, Josette disconnected the call and then dialed Seth at his office. Seth instructed the dazed Josette to take the train into the city and told her that he would be there waiting to drive her to Dr. Tucker's office. Josette backed the car out of the driveway and drove to the station. Leaving everything in the car, including the groceries, the dog food and the dry cleaning, she boarded a train into the city.

The diagnosis of cancer had come unexpectedly, right out of left field and, along with Seth and Dr. Tucker, the decision was made to treat it aggressively. Two days after diagnosis, she was admitted into the hospital and a radical surgery had been performed in which one of her ovaries was removed. The surgery was followed up with two months of radiation treatment, during which time Josette's glorious hair fell out in clumps, her skin grew ashen and dry, her weight dropped tremendously and she fell into a depression that threatened to take what little life was left in her away. It wasn't until Dr. Tucker ran a series of post-operation tests and determined that the cancer was all gone that Josette was able to entertain the notion she would make it. Slowly, she regrouped and got back to the business of living. Her children, who had suffered terribly during her illness, received all of her time and attention once more. Within five months she had completely recovered, appearing as if she had never been sick in the first place. However, always in the back of her mind from that moment forward was the nagging fear that the cancer could come back. Three years later, there were indications that that was precisely what had happened, and she was pushed to the verge of having a nervous break-down as she awaited the test results. Fortunately, the tumors found that time had been benign and she'd walked away with a clean bill of health. The fear, however, always remained, lingering at the back of her mind.

"Well, Josette, perimenopause is a condition that exists sometimes for as short a period as one year, or as long as between two and eight years. During that time, your menstrual cycle can change tremendously. You may have stopped seeing a monthly period for a very long time, but that does not mean that you are not still ovulating. You've told me that other than the missed menses, you've not experienced any other marked symptoms of menopause such as hot flashes, headaches, mood swings or depression, right?"

Josette shook her head dumbly.

"But the chemo?" she sputtered, still believing that there was some sort of mistake.

"As I told you back then, Josette, one of your ovaries was still in very good shape.… This despite the tumors and the radiation therapy. There was always the possibility, no matter how remote."

"But, Dr. Tucker, I mean…well, Seth and I…we don't…" Josette's voice trailed off as she thought back to the past couple of months.

With the exception of the past two weeks, during which Seth had been in Chicago on business, they had been going at one another like rabbits. Their passionate encounters consumed them two to three times each week. Now that they had rediscovered each other, they absolutely could not get enough of one another.

Suddenly, she remembered the cruise. Of course, that must have been when it had happened. Although there was no way to know for sure, she told herself that it was all the magic of that impromptu lovers' sojourn that had done it.

"Don't what, Josette?"

"I guess…we do. I'm forty-six years old," Josette said, more to herself than to the doctor.

He smiled at that.

"And still kicking," he said sympathetically.

Josette sat silently for a moment, the reality of the situation washing over her like a wave of frigid water.

"Dr. Tucker, are you sure?" she asked at last.

"All that I can say to you is congratulations, Josette. Now, I'm sure you and your husband need some time to digest this, but keep in mind that because of your age, this will be treated as a high-risk pregnancy. I'd like you to make an appointment with my receptionist to come back in a couple of weeks from now. I will want to monitor your progress closely and frequently."

Dr. Tucker prescribed vitamins for Josette, patted her softly on her back and left the room. After dressing herself by rote, Josette left the doctor's office in a stupor. She walked around midtown Manhattan oblivious to the sights and sounds around her. It was a miracle that she didn't trip and fall, bump into anyone or get hit by a moving vehicle, for she was in a vacuum and nothing else existed besides herself and the news that had just been delivered to her. Although her chocolate-brown shearling coat was wide open and her gloves remained stuffed in her pockets, she did not feel cold. She was numb, inside and out, as she meandered around the city aimlessly.

Finally, when her feet told her that she was tired and her stomach screamed for food, she stopped walking. Slowly, she came to her senses, as if awakening from a dream. She looked around and found that she was on 138th Street and Saint Nicholas Avenue. She had walked almost fifty blocks from her doctor's office. It was dark outside; nightfall had long ago descended on the city. She stepped into a tiny, cluttered bodega, suddenly overcome with nausea, where she purchased a box of saltine crackers and a twenty-ounce bottle of ginger ale. As she stood on the sidewalk outside of the store, tears swam in her eyes. She looked at the half-eaten cracker in her hand and the tears began to fall. The last time she had satiated nausea with crackers and ginger ale had been one of the most joyous times of her life. She had loved being pregnant with both of her children. She had embraced the morning sickness, the weight gain, the swollen feet, an overactive pituitary gland and the difficulty walking. She had been very sick with Simone, her first pregnancy, throwing up for almost the entire nine months. Yet nothing could dampen the joy she felt at the mere thought of being charged with the responsibility of serving as a vessel bringing life into the world. Her children had been planned and, therefore, they had been wanted. Would she feel the same way this time?

This time she had been caught unawares. She had been so sure that she was past the childbearing stage in her life. She had not had a period in almost a year. She had begun having mini-hot flashes, albeit very mild ones—nothing like what she had heard about from her mother and other older women. Still, all of the signs said that she was menopausal. She had thought there was no longer a need for her and Seth to use birth control. Surprise, surprise.

Seth. How would she tell him this news? How would he react? She was so filled with conflicting emotions that she could not begin to fathom how he would feel about it. Another baby at their age was the last thing that either of them expected. Why now? Just when they had begun to rediscover themselves and seemed to be shaping a brand-new life of passion and communication, God had unfolded another plan for them. After the cruise, Seth had started bringing home brochures for different places he wanted them to visit. His excitement was contagious and they'd sat for hours planning things to do and places to see together. Seth was finally following the suit of his fellow senior partners who had long since passed the mantle and reduced their working hours. Waters, McLean, Berber and Crawford was a prestigious law firm with quality litigators whom Seth and the other partners had groomed over the years. There was no reason for him to continue working such long hours, spearheading numerous cases at a time. He had begun restructuring his practice so that the lead associates on his cases could handle much of the day-to-day business, leaving him free to keep Josette in bed for a few hours in the morning, feeding her breakfast and dining on her loving or to drop by Josette's office in the middle of the day, with lunch in tow. They were like newlyweds and enjoying every minute they could find to be together. Now all of that would have to change. Again.

Josette hailed a taxi, fatigue demanding that she not take another step. After giving the driver the address to the Larchmont train station where she'd parked her car that morning, she sat back in silence, taking small sips from her bottle of soda. She leaned her head back against the seat and closed her moist eyes. Tears continued to escape her eyelids as her conflicted emotions tumbled inside. She thought about the twelve pounds she'd lost, realizing that all of that effort had been a waste of time. At her age she'd probably gain twice as much as she'd gained during her other two pregnancies. She had enjoyed the dance classes at Dyobi so much, having branched out to an elementary calypso class, as well. Between that, choir practice, social outings with Natalie and all of the quality time she and Seth had been sharing, her life was full and complete now. As the holidays approached, she was looking forward to having Simone and Marcus home, but she realized now that as much as she missed them, she was actually enjoying not having to mother them on a daily basis. She even laughed at herself sometimes when she thought about how distraught she had been when Marcus had first left home. And what about them? How would they handle having a new little brother or sister when they were practically adults themselves?

Chapter 13

By the time the taxi reached the train station, Josette was an utter mess. Inside of her own vehicle, she locked the doors, turned on the ignition and sat staring out into the almost-empty parking lot. Finally, she realized that she needed to get her head together. She opened the mirror on the visor and looked disgustingly at herself.

"All right, girl, snap out of it," she said to her reflection.

At that moment, an image of one of her clients popped into her head. Mrs. Carter was a forty-five-year-old woman with four kids and she had just escaped an abusive marriage after fifteen years of serving as her husband's punching bag. She'd walked out of a nice home, leaving everything behind, and had spent the last three months living with her children in a battered woman's shelter. Yet every time she came into the offices at New Hope, she wore a radiant smile and had a light shining in her eyes that was one of determination and purpose. If that woman could hold her head up and deal with life's ups and downs, who was Josette to fall apart when she had so much more? She told herself that she had no right to behave as if this were the end of the world when so many women were facing far greater trials.

She took a few deep breaths in an attempt to get herself together. When she'd finally managed to put her tears in check, she searched through the glove compartment, retrieving a handful of tissues, and blew her nose. She smoothed her ruffled hair, refreshed the faded wine-colored lipstick on her lips and pulled out of the lot. Seth was already home when she arrived five minutes later, his car parked in the driveway. Josette put a smile on her face and headed inside.

"Hey, baby," he said, smiling from his seat in the den.

She leaned down and kissed his forehead.

"Busy day?" he asked.

"Not really," Josette replied as she removed her coat.

"Oh. It's late. What, did you and Natalie decide to hang out a bit?"

"No, I, uh…I was out walking."

"What do you mean, out walking?" Seth asked.

He studied Josette's face for a moment, noticing for the first time that despite the minimal makeup, she was pale.

"Babe, are you feeling all right? You look a little discolored."

Seth rose from his chair and walked over to the sofa. He took a seat next to Josette, reaching out to feel her forehead. Looking down, he noticed the bottle of ginger ale sticking out of her bag.

"Don't tell me you've caught that stomach flu that's been going around. Damn near everyone in my office has that bug," Seth said. "Why don't you go upstairs and I'll put the teakettle on."

"No, I don't want any tea," Josette answered.

"How about some soup then? Do we have any more clam chowder?" he asked, rising from the sofa.

"No, Seth, we're all out. But, honey, I don't want any soup. Please…would you sit back down?"

Josette patted the cushion beside her, her gaze remaining fixed on his face.

Seth slowly returned to his seat, his concern mounting with each passing second. He realized that something much more serious than a stomach flu was going on, and he was certain that he didn't want to hear whatever it was that his wife was about to tell him. He took her hands in his, trying to prepare himself to be strong. Hoping that it was not as bad as his imagination was leading him to believe it was, he looked into her eyes and waited patiently for her to talk.

"Seth…I went to see Dr. Tucker today. I'd been feeling a little light-headed lately and since I was due for a checkup, anyway, I called his office this morning and the receptionist was able to fit me in this afternoon."

"What'd he say?" Seth asked.

His heart seemed to stop beating as he waited for Josette to deliver her news. He willed his mind to stay empty, devoid of the thoughts of what she could be about to tell him. His worst fear was that the cancer had returned. That period a few years back had been the darkest time in their lives. For his part, he had tried to be strong and supportive. He had never allowed Josette to see him break down, although there had been many times when he had done just that. The mere thought of losing her had been enough to bring him to his knees, his breathing becoming altered and his stomach heaving and threatening to expel its contents. He would lock himself in the bathroom and turn on the hot and cold faucets in the sink to full blast so that no one would hear him sobbing. Every time he would have one of these breakdowns, which would only last a few minutes, he would pull himself back together and emerge from the bathroom with a

bright, albeit fake, smile on his face. He would
return to his wife's bedside to rub her stomach,
which had been in a constant state of upheaval due
to the chemotherapy. Then he would make sure
that the kids had done their homework and gotten
their clothes ready for school the next day. He'd
order dinner for them, staying away from fast foods
as many times a week as he could, but they always
knew how to get something fried and greasy out of
him when they really wanted to. All of their lives
he'd never quite been able to get them into bed precisely at their bedtimes because they knew how to
work him for one more story, one more glass of
water or some other excuse. During that trying
time while Josette had recovered, they'd needed
constant reassuring from him and sometimes that
had meant sitting up with one or both of them at
night.

After securing the kids for the night and shutting
down the house, Seth would return to the master
bedroom to feed Josette from one of the hundred
containers of soup her mother had made and placed
in their deep freezer when she'd stayed with them
during Josette's hospitalization. If Josette was able
to keep the soup down, it would be a good night.
If not, he would help her bathe, change their bed
and climb in beside her to hold her in his arms all
night. He'd be so tired the next morning, but he
would get up and do it all over again, grateful that
he still had that opportunity. That had been the

scariest time in his life, and he had made all kinds of pacts with God. He'd promised that if Josette made it through this, he'd never ask for another thing. She had and, while he hated the thought of having to go back on his word, he was prepared to offer anything in exchange for her good health now.

"I don't really know how to tell you this, Seth, so I guess I'll just spit it out," Josette said.

She took a deep breath, looked into her husband's eyes and uttered the unthinkable.

"I'm pregnant," she said.

For a moment Seth sat looking blankly at her. It was as if she hadn't spoken. He continued staring at her, speechless. The ticking of the grandfather clock in the corner of the room was the only sound, save for their breathing.

"Did you hear me, Seth?" Josette asked at length.

"No…I don't think I did."

His mind could not wrap itself around what she'd said, part of his brain unable to decipher between the word *pregnant* and the word *cancer,* which seemed to have implanted itself there.

"Dr. Tucker said that I am healthy, in good shape and pregnant. The light-headedness, the nausea…it's because I'm pregnant. I'm going to have a baby."

"That's impossible," Seth said in a monotone voice.

"No, sweetie, it's actually not impossible. See, when a man and a woman—"

"Save the biology lesson, Josette. What I meant was, I thought you couldn't have any more kids. What with the chemotherapy and menopause…"

"I know. That's what I thought, too. Apparently, we both thought wrong."

"Josette, I don't understand this. What exactly did Dr. Tucker say?"

"Seth, what's not to understand? The doctor said that I'm pregnant. He did a blood test and there's no mistake."

Seth continued looking at Josette's pale face for a moment longer and then pulled his hands away from hers and stood up. He walked around the back of the sofa, stopping in front of the window for a moment. He ran his hand across the top of his head several times before resuming his pace. He stopped again in front of the fireplace, his back to Josette.

"Pregnant?" he asked, a rhetorical question for which he expected no answer.

Josette did not respond. She leaned back against the sofa, suddenly exhausted. She closed her eyes, her hands laced across her stomach. When she had discovered that she was pregnant with Simone, it had been very early in the pregnancy. Up until that point she had been very regular in her menstrual cycle and when it had been two weeks late in making an appearance, she'd known. Instantaneously, she'd begun to feel morning sickness and fatigue. By the time she'd gone to the doctor for the first time, it had been a mere confirmation of what she'd already known. She remembered how she'd come home from that doctor's visit and sat down at their kitchen table to wait for Seth. When he'd come in, she could hardly contain herself enough to get the words out. They had only been trying for a couple of months and her doctor had told her that it could take up to a year after ceasing the consumption of birth-control pills to become pregnant. Seth had sat down across the table from her and held her hands, just as he had done tonight. However, that time, when she'd told him the news, he had jumped up from the table, snatching her into his arms and lifting her into the air. By the time he'd let her down, tears were streaming down both of their cheeks. They'd made love that night and afterward he'd lain beside her and rubbed and kissed her belly until she'd fallen asleep.

"I can't believe this," Seth said.

"Yeah, well, I'm having a hard time with it myself," Josette answered sarcastically.

Still filled with ambivalent emotions herself, the last thing she needed was to hear her own dismay reflected in Seth's voice. She sat up, looking at Seth, who had turned to face her. Another look at her pale face, her tight expression, and he knew that it was true.

"I don't know what to say, Josette."

"How do you feel about this?"

"I really don't know how to answer that question. This was certainly not what I expected to hear from you tonight. I thought we were going to put the finishing touches on our vacation to Hawaii or Europe.... Now this."

Seth's voice was elevated, and he fought hard to control himself. He didn't know how to articulate to her the mixture of emotions he was feeling, anger being the most prevalent. He felt cheated. Just when he was getting his wife back, here she was being snatched away from him again.

"Why are you yelling, Seth?" Josette asked.

"I'm not yelling," Seth snapped.

Josette rose from the sofa, picked up her bag from the floor where she'd laid it and turned away from Seth. She began walking out of the room, propelled by will more than strength.

"Where are you going?" he asked her back.

"To bed. I'm tired, and I'm not up for this tonight," she said over her shoulder.

Seth watched her walk away, listened as heavy steps took her up to their bedroom. He knew that he should stop her and say something else, but he couldn't make himself do it. He paced around the den for a while longer, attempted to sit down in his armchair and watch television, but felt restless and uneasy. He wanted to go upstairs and hold his wife. In his heart he knew that that was where he should be, but he could not make himself go up those stairs. He was afraid that she would see right through him and he didn't want to take that chance. Right now, he needed time alone. He needed to feel his anger and disappointment, to process it and deal with it before he tried to deal with whatever it was that Josette was feeling.

Seth poured himself a glass of Grand Marnier and took a hefty swig. He really didn't intend to get drunk because he knew that was a lesser man's response to stress, but he needed to do something to take the edge off his nerves. Two hours later, however, an empty bottle sat beside a sleeping Seth. Josette returned to the den to find her husband passed out on the sofa. She picked up the empty glass and bottle from the floor and sucked her teeth, thinking that it must be nice to have the option to get shit-faced when confronted with a problem. She, unfortunately, did not have that luxury.

Josette toyed with the idea of leaving him there to sleep uncomfortably on the sofa in his clothes, but couldn't do it. She called his name a few times to rouse him, shaking his shoulder roughly, and then helped Seth to his feet. In the bedroom, she helped him out of his clothes and when she'd finally settled him onto the bed, he pulled her down with him. He wrapped his arms around her body and fell asleep against her, inhaling her scent. Josette lay awake for a long time, hoping that tomorrow would be as peaceful as these twilight hours.

Chapter 14

Seth poured another capful of body soap into the palms of his hands and rubbed them together. He rubbed the lather onto Josette's shoulders. They were seated in the master bedroom's hot tub, amid warm water and whirring bubbles. It had been days since they'd discovered that they were going to be parents for the third time and, while tension still rested between them, for the time being it had been relegated to a corner of the room to be dealt with later.

"You didn't eat anything tonight," Seth observed.

"I'm not hungry. The mere thought of food makes me queasy," Josette responded.

"Can't Dr. Tucker give you anything for that? I mean, times have changed in the past twenty years. You'd think they'd have figured out a way to make women more comfortable."

"You'd think, but unfortunately, that's not the case. I'm going in to see him next week so I'll talk to him about it, not that it'll do any good."

With soapy washcloth in hand, Seth reached around and washed Josette's breasts and stomach. He loved bathing her, enjoying the way her skin felt against his and especially loving to caress the folds of her body. He passed the washcloth across her stomach, remembering how it had expanded as the months had progressed during her prior two pregnancies. He had marveled at a woman's body's ability to stretch to accommodate a developing life. He had loved to touch her protruding belly, to feel the skin growing tight over their baby. He was not sure that he would be able to feel the same way this time when her pregnancy began to show. In his heart he believed that a child deserved to be surrounded by love and acceptance from the moment of conception, but knowing something and being able to feel it were two entirely different ends of the spectrum.

He leaned forward and kissed Josette's cheek and neck. He said a silent prayer, asking for strength and fortitude as he waited for his heart to feel what his mind told him he should feel. He hoped that the love he had for his wife and his family would be enough to carry them all through this.

Josette knew that Seth was struggling with this latest development in their lives. Were it not for her own misgivings, she might have been able to comfort him and ease his fears. With each passing day, she felt the distance between them widening as they each became lost in their own uncertainties.

The pregnancy was advancing and, as the inexplicable fatigue set in, Josette was having a hard time keeping up with her daily routine. She knew that with her advanced age, she would probably have a harder time than she'd had before. She spent her days locked inside of her office, most of the time munching on crackers and tea biscuits, which she kept inside a desk drawer. They seemed to keep the nausea at bay for short intervals—long enough for her to get some work done. It wasn't long, however, before Natalie began to notice changes in her.

"So what gives, Ms. Josette?" she asked one day over sandwiches at the office.

"What are you talking about?" Josette replied as she picked apart her sandwich.

Natalie watched her remove the tomatoes, the onions and the cheese from her bread, close the sandwich up and take a tiny bite.

"Well, for starters, why are you picking apart your food like that?"

"Hmm?" Josette asked. "Oh, I just don't feel like eating all of that today."

"Yeah, right. You've been holed up in your office all day, every day for the past couple of weeks, you barely eat and, don't take this the wrong way, sweetie, but you look torn up."

"Oh yeah, I won't take that the wrong way!" Josette replied.

Natalie just looked at her, her lips twisted in an expression that told her the cat was out of the bag.

"All right. Close the door," Josette whispered.

Natalie jumped up and shut the door to Josette's office. She returned to her seat and waited for Josette's bombshell.

"I went to my doctor a couple of weeks ago and…well, you're not going to believe this. I could hardly believe it, but, it's true. I don't know how this happened.… Well, I do know, but I just really didn't expect it—"

"Josette, would you spit it out already," Natalie commanded, the anticipation driving her into a frenzy.

"I'm pregnant."

"What?" Natalie asked. "That's impossible," she added.

"Why does everyone keep saying that? It is apparently very possible and very much happening."

"Wow! Isn't that something. So I guess you and Seth got your groove back after all, huh?" Natalie giggled.

"Chuckle, chuckle. I'm glad you find amusement at my expense."

"I'm sorry, Josette, but you've got to admit that this is a little bit ironic. So, have you told Seth?"

"Yes, he knows."

"Humph. By the way you say that I take it that's a sore subject."

Josette spent the next few minutes filling Natalie in on the precarious position that she and Seth now found themselves in. The strain between them came more from what they didn't say, hadn't yet found the words to say, than from anything they said or did.

"So what are you going to do?" Natalie asked.

"About what?"

"About the pregnancy, of course. Are you going to go through with it?"

Josette looked at Natalie as if she had two heads.

"What on earth kind of question is that?"

"Oh, Josette, don't be so naive. Women get pregnant every day and, for a variety of reasons, many of them decide to terminate their pregnancies. It is an option, you know, and unless the right-wing conservatives have their way, we will always have that option."

"I could never do that," Josette said, her hand pressed against her chest and her eyes as huge as saucers.

"I'm sorry. I didn't realize you were anti-abortion. I didn't mean to offend you," Natalie apologized sincerely.

"I'm not anti-abortion, if that's what's right for

someone else. It's just not something *I* could ever do. That's just never been a consideration for me."

"Well, I guess you're lucky then," Natalie said quietly.

"What do you mean, Natalie?"

"Oh, nothing. Forget about it."

Josette could tell that the conversation had stirred up something distressing for Natalie. She reached across the desk and took her hand.

"Do you want to talk about it?" she asked simply.

Natalie looked at her friend for a moment, a wan smile appearing on her lips.

"It was a long, long time ago. I…I'm over it. It happened, and I did what I had to do."

"You had an abortion?" Josette asked.

"Yeah. I was seventeen and stupid. I don't regret it for one minute though. I was in no position to be having a baby, especially not with a boy who was more interested in video games and chasing skirts than being somebody's husband and father. We stayed together for about five minutes after the abortion, and every day I thank my lucky stars that I was smart enough not to bring a child into this world back then, under those circumstances."

"I'm sorry you had to go through that, Natalie," Josette said, rubbing the back of Natalie's hand.

"Yeah, well, you live and you learn. Now I have a wonderful husband and a healthy, happy little boy. So all's well that ends well."

"That's true. I just know that, for me at least…well, I don't know how you can be so matter-of-fact about it. I mean, I know that as hard as the situation is, terminating a pregnancy has got to make you feel pretty bad."

"Yes, Josette, it's not an easy thing to live with, but what about having a baby when you don't want it? I know that this has got to be hard for you guys to face."

Josette wrapped the remnants of her sandwich back into the plastic in which it had come, unable to stomach any more of it.

"It is, but I can't even comprehend the alternative. Seth and I have faced tougher situations before and we've survived them. Besides, how could we not want our own baby, even if we didn't plan it?"

"Well, girl, then all that's left to say is a heartfelt congratulations!" Natalie exclaimed.

She jumped up from her seat, zipped around the desk and wrapped her arms around Josette. Giving her a big squeeze, she squealed with delight.

"Ooh, now you know godmommy Natalie is going to spoil this little crumb-snatcher rotten."

"I know you will." Josette laughed.

The women chattered conspiratorially for the remainder of their lunch hour and for the first time since discovering that she was pregnant, Josette stopped worrying and started enjoying the idea that she would once again be a part of the miracle of birth and creating new life. She talked about whether she wanted another girl or another boy, and was ultimately unable to decide. All she truly cared about was that she would have a healthy baby that both she and Seth would come to love and cherish.

to see. He would be at her side, comforting her,
reassuring that the world had, in reality, not
changed, and their love would conquer love, pain . . .

Chapter 15

Seth leaned against the brick building, glanced at his
watch and looked up and down the street, first to the
left and then to the right. It was not like Josette to be
late for an appointment, and despite the fact that it was
merely five minutes past their four o'clock appointment with Dr. Tucker, he was concerned. Josette was
the type of person who arrived at least ten to fifteen
minutes early for any engagement, from movie dates
to seminars. She'd once told him that whenever she
was meeting someone, especially if it were for the
first time, she loved to watch the person approach.
She claimed you could tell a lot about a person from
his or her stride and the way he or she entered a room.

He remembered their first date as if it were yesterday. He was running late, a habit which took years of being married to Josette to break. They'd been were students at UCLA, she a sophomore and he a junior. Having been raised in the old-fashioned ways, he had wanted to pick her up for their date from her dorm, but she'd insisted that they meet at a coffeehouse right outside of campus. Initially, he thought that she was reluctant to tell him where she lived, being skeptical of his motives, but he later understood things better when she explained her *early arrival* ideology.

He drove his raggedy brown 1964 Chevy Impala from the other side of campus since he was unsure if she'd want to go anywhere else besides the coffee shop. He parked in the nearest available spot, which was across the street. At six o'clock on a Friday evening, traffic was pretty heavy on the boulevard, so he had to wait several minutes before being able to cross the busy street. While he stood waiting for an opening, he adjusted the collar of his button-down shirt, first opening and then reclosing the top button. He patted the right breast of his blazer to be sure that his wallet was safely tucked inside. He smoothed his bushy eyebrows, cupped his left hand and blew into it to check the freshness of his breath. He reached inside his right jacket pocket, retrieved an opened pack of Violet candies, popped one in his mouth, then another. Unbeknownst to him, Josette sat watching him from inside the coffee shop from the moment he'd placed his car in Park.

By the time Seth finally made it across the street, Josette had already fallen in love with him. Of course, she did not let him in on this startling fact until several months after they had been dating. She told him that she'd learned more about him in those three or four minutes of watching him prepare to meet her than she had during their ensuing date. For him, he was a goner the day he first met her and asked her to go out with him. She was working in the campus bookstore and helped him place an order for an out-of-stock textbook on business ethics. Her pretty face and diminutive figure paled in comparison to her sweet smile and disposition. He'd stayed in that bookstore for an hour, talking with her between customers and laughing harder than he'd ever remembered laughing. She'd been funny and witty, and he absolutely could not believe his good fortune in meeting her.

Twenty-odd years later, she still held the key to his heart. He knew that he'd been less than supportive since this latest pregnancy, but his love for her was unchanged. That was one reason why he'd invited himself along for her doctor's appointment. He had yet to figure out why fate had decided to send them on this path again, but whatever the reason, he had no right to question it. He'd have to suck up his disappointment and find a way to accept the situation as it was. He wanted Josette to know that their marriage vows were still sacred to him. He was by her side, for richer and poorer, for better and worse, through sickness and in health, for as long as he lived.

He looked up toward Madison Avenue, the direction he expected she'd come from, and spotted her waiting at the light. His Diahann-Carroll-Lena-Horne. He studied her from head to toe. *Polished, graceful* and *serene* were the words that came to mind. He loved that she had taken to wearing her hair down again recently, reveling in the way it framed her face, the feel and smell of it when he was near her. Soon she'd begin to fill out; her five-foot-five-inch frame would seem shorter as the pregnancy added pounds to her body. He had enjoyed her pregnancies, both of them. She'd seemed even more sensual then, if that was possible. He remembered with fondness that, during the last few weeks of pregnancy, when intercourse had become awkward or uncomfortable for her, he'd enjoyed orally stimulating her to climax. Even though her huge belly had prevented him from seeing her face easily as he'd dined on her, her moans and soft squeals had driven him to ecstasy every time. Maybe this wouldn't be so bad after all.

"Hey, sorry I'm late. Minor crisis at the office," Josette said as she approached.

Seth took her arm at the elbow, leaned down and kissed her warmly on the lips.

"Don't worry about it. I haven't been waiting long."

He opened the lobby door for her and followed her inside. They stopped at the reception desk, where Josette signed in and presented her insurance information. They took seats in a colorful waiting room where two other patients were already seated.

"So what was the crisis?" Seth asked.

"A young mother whom we helped get situated in her own place a few months ago made a huge mistake. She felt bad that her ex hadn't seen the baby in a while so she agreed to let him come by her apartment up in Harlem. We purposely tell these women not to give out their addresses and, if necessary, to only meet their former partners in public places, but sometimes they just don't listen."

"What happened?"

"Well, he came and things went okay at first, but when it was time to leave, he started in on her and she got scared and picked up the phone to call the police. That apparently really ticked him off and he hit her."

"Coward," Seth growled.

"Yeah, well, one thing that bastard wasn't counting on was that in the four months that they'd been apart, she'd really decided that she wasn't going to be his victim anymore. This time she hit him back. She actually picked up one of her son's toy trucks and knocked the living hell out of him.

Then she grabbed the baby and hightailed it out of that apartment. She took the subway downtown and, not knowing where else to go, she came to the office."

"Humph," Seth said. "You didn't have any trouble from that jerk did you?"

"No, no. By the time we calmed her down and got the whole story from her, we figured the best thing to do was to have the police check the apartment out. Do you know that fool had the nerve to still be there? They walk in and he's sitting at her kitchen table, holding a dish towel to his bleeding head and acting like it was the most natural thing in the world! They took his butt out of there in cuffs, even after he started screaming about his being the victim and whatnot."

"The cops certainly don't go for that crap. A brother could be lying there bleeding with his thing in his hand, à la Lorena Bobbitt, and the first question they ask is 'What'd you do to her?'" Seth laughed.

"Ain't that the truth," Josette agreed, laughing. "Anyway, we got in touch with her sister. She came, picked her and the baby up and took them home. I tell you…I'm certainly glad that all days aren't this dramatic because I don't think I could take it."

"Are you feeling okay?" Seth asked.

"Yeah, I'm fine. Actually, dealing with all of that mess took my mind away from thoughts of vomiting for a while, which was a nice reprieve," Josette revealed with a chuckle.

Twenty minutes later, they were called in to see the doctor. Seth waited outside of the lavatory while Josette delivered a urine sample and changed into a cloth gown. He accompanied her into the examination room where a nurse took her weight and blood pressure. A technician then set up the sonogram machine and prepared Josette for the doctor to perform the procedure. He opened her gown at the waist, rubbed a cold, clear jelly across her abdomen and lowered the bed so that she was lying flat on her back. When Dr. Tucker entered the room, the technician lowered the lights and handed the instrument over to him.

"All right, Miss Josette, let's see what's going on here. Mr. Crawford, I know you're probably a pro at this by now, so why don't you tell me…do you see anything?"

Seth studied the screen, looking for signs of his baby, but was uncertain if the shades of gray and black were boy, girl or Josette's intestines. Dr. Tucker laughed when Seth shared his confusion with him.

"Don't worry, Mr. Crawford, I won't take your license away from you for that. Okay, let's see. Well, I can see why you're having difficulty. It appears that you are very early in the pregnancy, Josette," he said as he returned the instrument to its receptacle.

The doctor began to tap and press against Josette's abdomen, moving his hands around to various positions.

"Based on the size of your uterus at this point and the physical symptoms you've been having, I'd say you're somewhere between three and five weeks. Does that sound about right with you folks?"

Seth looked to Josette for official confirmation of the doctor's estimation, as he, too, was convinced that conception had taken place during their recent trip to the Mexican Riviera.

"Yes, Dr. Tucker. That sounds right," he answered.

"All right. Well, the pictures are a little difficult to read and that's probably due to the relatively early stage of the pregnancy as well as the baby's position. What I'd like to do is wait another three to four weeks and try again. How does that sound to you?"

"That's fine, Dr. Tucker."

"Good, good. Otherwise, how have you been feeling?" he asked.

The technician turned the lights on and left the room. Dr. Tucker retrieved Josette's chart from the table beside him and began scratching notes on it.

"I've been just fine...pregnant, of course, but not doing too badly," Josette said.

"Actually, Doctor, she's been very sick.... Sicker than I remember her being before—either time,"

Seth chimed in, his thick eyebrows knotted in concern.

"Is it just nausea or are you vomiting, too?" Dr. Tucker asked.

"A little of both, but really, it's not that bad. I mean, a little constipation and minor cramping, but really nothing for me to complain about," Josette insisted.

"Well, it looks like you've only gained a couple of pounds since I saw you two weeks ago. I'd like you to take it easy. Sleep when you feel tired.... Stay home from work when you're not feeling up to it. Seth, I know I don't have to tell you that Daddy's job right now is to make sure that Mommy rests and eats."

Seth nodded.

Before they left the doctor's office he provided Seth and Josette with literature written for people who were becoming parents later in life. They had thought they'd already learned all there was to know about childbirth during the first two pregnancies, but to their surprise, because of their ages, there would be some dramatic differences this time around. One such contrast was the fact that Josette would have to undergo an amniocentesis, a reality that terrified her. The thought of a long, thin, hollow needle being inserted through her abdomen into the amniotic sack to extract fluid scared her out of her wits. While she understood that it was impor-tant to make sure that the baby was not affected by some of the life-threatening maladies that could occur in a high-risk pregnancy such as this, that knowledge did not make her feel any better about the procedure.

Chapter 16

Josette alternated between mashing the yams she was using to make her pies and walking to the front door and peering through the glass as she anxiously awaited Marcus's arrival. Against her wishes, he had insisted on driving home for Christmas break instead of flying because he didn't want to be in town for four weeks without his truck. It had snowed heavily the day before, dumping six to eight inches between Washington, D.C. and New York. Today, the winds were high and there was a forty-percent chance that it would snow again before nightfall. The fact that he was driving through those elements kept Josette on edge all day.

Simone had arrived from school two days ago and was currently at the mall doing some last-minute shopping. It was Christmas eve and, while Josette usually enjoyed the holidays immensely, the tension between her and Seth made this holiday less exciting for her than ever before. He was currently holed up in the den, reviewing documents for a cumbersome case his firm had taken on. At least that was what he'd told her, but she suspected that he was also trying to avoid her.

Josette sighed deeply, absently rubbing her hand across her belly. There had been no expansion in her midsection as yet, but knowing that the baby was there, growing inside her, was strangely comforting. By six o'clock in the evening, Josette had two potato pies in the oven, the ingredients for a carrot cake prepared and waiting to be mixed together and baked, and a ham that was decorated with cloves, pineapples and her special glaze, and would go into the oven first thing in the morning. She turned off the flame under a huge pot of collard greens made with smoked turkey and extra crushed red peppers because Marcus loved them spicy. Her zesty potato salad made with red potatoes was chilling in the refrigerator. She'd scaled Christmas dinner down at Seth's request, who hadn't wanted her to tire herself out making a signature seven-course meal. Tomorrow, Seth would take care of baking the ham and heating the other courses. He also planned to make baked macaroni and cheese, for which Simone had already boiled the noodles and cut up the mixed cheddar cheese. Simone's job would be the biscuits made from scratch using Seth's grandmother's recipe.

Had Marcus been home earlier, he would have cut the collard greens from the stalks, peeled the potatoes and done all of the other preparatory work. That was his favorite part of helping out in the kitchen, and as it was Josette's least favorite part, they made the perfect team. Here again was that familiar pang of longing she'd felt off and on since Marcus's departure for school in September. It had been really bad at first, but she'd worked hard to cast it aside. Once she'd begun dancing, singing and doing other things for herself, she'd found that instead of a longing, it was more of a nostalgic sensation. When she and Seth had rekindled their flame, she'd finally started to enjoy the fact that her children were off on their own and she did not have to worry about their needs on a day-to-day basis.

The distance between her and Seth right now seemed to bring all her progress to a halt and once again she was feeling the pain of having an empty nest. However, the fact was that it wasn't quite so empty anymore. She rubbed her hand across her belly again. The flash of headlights across the kitchen window drew her attention. She wiped her hands on a light-blue dish towel and hurried out of the room. She peered through the window, spotting Marcus's TrailBlazer as it came to a halt next to her

KIMANI PRESS™

An Important Message from the Publisher

Dear Reader,

Because you've chosen to read one of our fine novels, I'd like to say "thank you"! And, as a special way to say thank you, I'm offering to send you two Kimani Romance™ novels and two surprise gifts – absolutely FREE! These books will keep it real with true-to-life African-American characters that turn up the heat and sizzle with passion.

Please enjoy the free books and gifts with our compliments...

Linda Gill

Publisher, Kimani Press

Peel off Seal and Place Inside...

We'd like to send you two free books to introduce you to our new line – Kimani Romance™! These novels feature strong, sexy women and African-American heroes that are charming, loving and true. Our authors fill each page with exceptional dialogue, exciting plot twists, and enough sizzling romance to keep you riveted until the very end!

KIMANI ROMANCE ... LOVE'S ULTIMATE DESTINATION

Your two books have a combined cover price of $11.98 in the U.S. and $13.98 in Canada, but are yours **FREE!** We'l even send you two wonderful surprise gifts. You can't lose!

EDITOR'S "THANK YOU" FREE GIFTS GUIDE

Two NEW Kimani Romance™ Novels
Two exciting surprise gifts

I have placed my Editor's "Thank You" Free Gifts seal in the space provided at right. Please send me 2 FREE books, and my 2 FREE Mystery Gifts. I understand that I am under no obligation to purchase anything further, as explained on the back of this card.

PLACE
FREE GIFTS
SEAL
HERE

168 XDL ELWZ   368 XDL ELXZ

FIRST NAME

LAST NAME

ADDRESS

APT.#

CITY

STATE/PROV.

ZIP/POSTAL CODE

Thank You!

Offer limited to one per household and not valid to current subscribers of Kimani Romance.
Your Privacy – Kimani Press is committed to protecting your privacy. Our Privacy Policy is available online at www.eHarlequin.com or upon request from the Reader Service. From time to time we make our lists of customers available to reputable firms who may have a product or service of interest to you. If you would prefer for us not to share your name and address, please check here. ☐

If offer card is missing write to: The Reader Service, 3010 Walden Ave., P.O. Box 1867, Buffalo, NY 14240-1867

BUSINESS REPLY MAIL
FIRST-CLASS MAIL   PERMIT NO. 717-003   BUFFALO, NY

POSTAGE WILL BE PAID BY ADDRESSEE

THE READER SERVICE
3010 WALDEN AVE
PO BOX 1867
BUFFALO NY 14240-9952

NO POSTAGE
NECESSARY
IF MAILED
IN THE
UNITED STATES

car in the driveway. She flung the front door open, clapping her hands twice with excitement.

"Hey, Ma," Marcus boomed as he climbed out of the vehicle. She could swear he'd gotten taller and bigger in the three months that he'd been away. In a quick leap and bound he was across the lawn and had scooped her tiny frame up into his big arms, lifting her off the ground.

"Marcus, put me down," she squealed like a delighted child.

Marcus swung her around once again and then returned her to her feet. With his arm around her shoulder, he led her into the house. Seth, having heard Josette's excited screams, was drawn from the den and met them in the front hall.

"Well, well, man. I was beginning to think you weren't coming at all," he said, extending his hand to his son.

Marcus released Josette briefly, grabbing his father's hand in his. The two men embraced, patting one another on the back heartily.

"Pops, you know I wouldn't miss Christmas for anything."

Seth stepped back, admiring his son. He still couldn't believe that this was the same little wrinkled baby whose umbilical cord he himself had severed, separating him from his mother's body. His red face had been contorted with wailing cries as the nurse had wrapped him in a blanket and handed him over to Seth. Seth had held him, practically in one hand, and looked down into that face simply awestruck. Now, Marcus was almost bigger than his father. Seth reconciled himself to the fact that his son was a man, which was not an easy task at all.

"Where are your things?" Josette asked.

"They're in the car. I'll get 'em later. I'm hungry. I know you got something cooked up in here," Marcus said, his voice trailing behind him as he headed toward the kitchen.

"What else is new?" Josette said, following him. "Uh-uh, hands off of that. I only boiled that ham— I didn't bake it yet," she scolded.

She stepped around Marcus and reached into the refrigerator, removing the plastic bowl she'd set aside for him earlier. She pulled the top off the bowl and handed it over to him.

"Now that's what I'm talking about," Marcus said as he spied the beef stew, white rice and string beans in the bowl.

He stuck the bowl in the microwave and then turned to the sink, where he squeezed out some Palmolive and washed his hands under the faucet. Josette shook her head, knowing that no matter how many times she told her kids not to wash their hands in the kitchen sink but to go to the bathroom, they would continue to do it. Some things just never changed.

Seth was leaning against the kitchen's entryway, still marveling at his son.

"So how was the drive?" he asked.

"Not bad. The roads were pretty clear until we hit the New Jersey Turnpike and then I guess because it's so cold up here, it was a little icy. Christian was driving at that point, but I had to take over because he was clutching the steering wheel like a scared old lady. Traffic got a little backed up...but it wasn't too bad."

"I still don't know why you insisted upon driving all the way up here. You know you could have just driven my car or your dad's while you were here."

"Come on, Ma. I need my whip," Marcus said.

A short time later, Simone came in from her mall outing, laden with shopping bags and fast-food containers. Josette wanted to warn her that all the junk food she ate would catch up to her in a few years, turning her curvaceous size-four body into one with dimples and rolls where there shouldn't be any. However, she knew that it wouldn't do any good because at Simone's age it is difficult to believe that one day youth will be a distant memory. The best Josette could do would be to make sure she kept both of the kids so full of her home cooking while they were home that they wouldn't have room for that junk.

Seth and Josette had decided to wait until after Christmas dinner to tell the kids about the baby. By that time, one or both of them might notice how little Josette was eating or that the pallor of her skin was not quite her normal coloring.

Josette had covered the dining-room table with her favorite holiday tablecloth, made of gold lace with a scalloped trim. She had also covered the six wrought-iron chair backs with gold chair covers. Ivory candles with specks of gold in them adorned the table's flower centerpiece and holiday tunes issued from the stereo speakers. The Crawford home was filled with the holiday spirit and this spirit even served to melt some of the frost that had settled between Seth and Josette.

Dinner stretched on for hours and was filled with laughter and merriment; the family truly enjoyed being together again under one roof.

"Oh, Ma, Aunt Carmelita called while you were napping this afternoon. I forgot to tell you," Simone informed her.

Carmelita was Josette's sister, the baby of the family. In her late thirties, Carmelita was twice divorced and still searching for Mr. Right. She had one child, a son, who at age nine had begun acting out terribly in school and was now currently living with her first ex-husband. Despite the fact that the man had made a lousy husband, he was a great father and had managed to turn the boy around. Josette suspected that many of the boy's problems stemmed from his hatred of Carmelita's second husband, but Carmelita was not willing to hear that theory. Husband number two had lasted a mere three years, two of which had been spent between the emergency room and the police station. It had been more like a drawn-out Ali and Frazier main attraction than a marriage. Josette loved her sister to death, but she was glad that she kept her drama out there in Arizona where she lived.

"What's she up to?" Josette asked.

"Said she's spending Christmas in Jamaica. She'll be back on the third and will call you then."

"Jamaica, huh? I wonder what his name is," Seth mumbled.

Josette started to say something in defense of her sister but realized that he was absolutely right, so she didn't.

"Uncle Nardo sent you guys a couple of envelopes. They're on the mantel near the tree," Josette said, changing the subject.

Whenever her brother managed to be in town for the holidays, he would spend Christmas or New Year's Eve or both with them. The kids got a big kick out of him, and he and Seth were more like brothers than brothers-in-law. Unfortunately, this year he was in Singapore on business and didn't expect to be back until the end of January. Suddenly, she missed her brother and couldn't wait until his return. She could see the expression on his face now when she told him she was pregnant, and while he would think she was absolutely nuts for having another baby at this stage, he would be happy for her. He'd always doted on his niece and nephew, often taking them for long weekends, and they adored him.

Over warm pie and French vanilla ice cream, Josette delivered the news to Simone and Marcus.

"Guys, Dad and I have some news," she began hesitantly.

She felt nervous, as if she were about to confess to her mother that she was no longer a virgin. She took a deep breath and looked to Seth, who at that point was looking down into the bottom of his empty wineglass as if there were room in it for him to climb. She realized that he would not be of any help to her on this one, and she forged ahead alone.

"What's up, Ma? Is everything all right?" Marcus asked as he spooned another helping of ice cream on top of his pie.

Simone looked worriedly from one parent to another. Being the eldest, she remembered well when her mother had been ill from the cancer in her ovary, and that feeling of constant terror had stayed fresh in her mind over the years.

"Actually, everything is great. There is really no easy way for me to say this, so I'll just say it. Your dad and I are expecting a baby," she finished, looking from one child to the other.

Both of the Crawford children looked at their mother, the power of speech eluding them momentarily. They studied her serious expression, the expectant smile that skirted on her lips, and then turned to their father. His smile was weak, and as they waited for him to say something that contradicted the news their mother had just delivered, they soon realized that they were waiting in vain. Finally, Simone and Marcus looked at one another, but each failed to provide the answer that the other was looking for.

"Is anyone going to say anything?" Josette asked.

"Uh…well…I don't really know what to say. Did you guys plan this?" Simone asked finally.

"No, not exactly. It wasn't at all something we were expecting…. We didn't really think it was possible—"

"Ma, aren't you the one always telling us to make sure it's wrapped up?" Marcus laughed.

Suddenly, his laughter grew contagious, spreading around the room until everyone was cracking up hysterically. Through the fits of laughter, Josette explained that the pregnancy had been discovered by her doctor during a checkup and that he'd assured her that despite the fact that she was a forty-six-year-old cancer survivor, the odds were still extremely good that she would have a problem-free pregnancy.

Surprisingly, both of the kids seemed to take the news well. Josette couldn't help but notice that their happiness over the prospect of a new baby in the house seemed to have some effect on Seth. He joked with Marcus that if it was a boy, maybe he'd finally have some real competition on the asphalt. Finally, Josette excused herself. She had been following Dr.

Tucker's rest orders really well and at the first sign of fatigue she made every effort to take a rest. Simone followed her upstairs and helped her into bed.

"I'm not a crippled old woman, Simone. I'm just pregnant, and I'm not even showing yet," she complained, although secretly enjoying being fussed over by her daughter.

"I know, but I'm not going to be around here much until the summer so let me take care of you now, okay?"

"Fine, have it your way. You know, you guys had better be careful, because I could really get used to being pampered."

"Well, you would deserve it...the way you take care of everyone else all the time," Simone said, fluffing her mother's pillows beneath her. "Now, get some sleep and don't even think about getting up in the morning to make breakfast. I got it covered," she said, kissing her mother's forehead.

As Simone turned out the light and closed the door softly behind her, Josette was already slipping away into peaceful slumber.

Chapter 17

The remainder of the kids' time at home was extra special—or at least it seemed so to Josette, who was at her best when being a mother hen. Simone and Marcus took turns making breakfast most mornings and even shared the task of a few dinners. Some nights Seth brought takeout in with him or alternatively, they all went out to eat. On New Year's Eve, Simone invited her new boyfriend over to meet the family. Josette had known that part of the reason why Simone had been so busy this past school semester and had rarely come home to visit had less to do with working, classes and organizations, and more to do with this young man.

However, she didn't push the issue, figuring that if she knew her daughter at all, the last thing Simone would be planning to do would be to get serious. Simone had always been a big flirt. The kind of girl who loved attention, but didn't go out of her way to get it or to keep it. Throughout high school there had been many boys sniffing around and she'd dated, but no one had ever lasted more than a few weeks. When she'd first left for college, Josette had sat her down for that special conversation and Simone had been very candid. She'd told her that while she was, in fact, still a virgin, she didn't know if she'd wait until marriage as her mother had done. Simone's philosophy was that a person didn't know for sure if they would ever get married and, therefore, that shouldn't be the brass ring to strive for. She intended to wait until she was in love before making that leap. She did reassure Josette that, to date, she had not been in love, but she was sure that she'd know it when she found it.

Josette had been satisfied with that answer and was certain that her daughter would make a wise decision in that regard. That was why it was with pleasure and apprehension that she now stood shaking the hand of the young man who seemed to have captured her daughter's attention in more than a passing fancy.

"Connor, it is a pleasure to meet you," Josette said. "Come in."

"Thank you, Mrs. Crawford. Wow, you guys have a beautiful home," he said.

Connor stood at about six feet five inches, taller than both Seth and Marcus. He was slimmer than both of them and his dark skin was as smooth as rich fudge. As Josette closed the door behind him, she gave Simone an approving wink. Her daughter definitely had good taste.

Connor kissed Simone on the cheek, one hand on her shoulder. The subtle intimacy in his gesture told Josette all that she needed to know.

"Simone's father and brother went out to the store, but they should have been back by now," Josette said, glancing nervously at her watch.

"Come on, Connor, you can help us in the kitchen."

The three of them headed into the kitchen where Josette resumed sitting on a stool watching Simone make a strawberry cheesecake. Simone put Connor to work whipping the cream cheese and butter while she worked on the crust.

"So, Connor, you're from South Jersey originally?"

"No, ma'am. Actually I was born in Virginia, right outside of Richmond. We moved to Jersey when I was about eleven years old. My dad was in the service back then. He was an engineering specialist and they needed teachers up at Fort Dix in Burlington County."

"I see. Is he retired now?"

"Yep. He did twenty years for Uncle Sam and now he owns his own electrical engineering contracting company down in Ocean County where we live."

"That's nice. And what about your mom?"

"She's a nurse—occupational therapy. Most of her patients are at home and she goes in a few times each week and cares for them. She loves it."

"Connor, add another tablespoon of margarine to that, please," Simone instructed.

"Simone tells me that you run a social-services agency, Mrs. Crawford."

"Yes, New Hope. I'm the director of a talented staff of people who do what we can to try to help women get back on their feet after crises."

The longer they continued chatting, the more Josette liked the young man. He was personable and humorous, reminding her of Seth in some ways. She knew instantly why Simone liked him so much. Just as the cheesecake was slid into the oven, the front door opened, bringing the long-lost Crawford men home.

"We were about to send the dog out to look for you two," Josette called.

Marcus bounded into the kitchen, bringing a cold breeze with him. He carried two heavy, black plastic bags. Seth lumbered behind, his hands full as well with white paper shopping bags.

"What is all of that?" Simone asked.

"Dad decided instead of getting Chinese food as planned that we should drive all the way down to the Crab House for dinner. We've got everything from stuffed lobster tails to oysters on the half shell!"

"Seth, you didn't have to go to all that trouble," Josette said as she began picking through the bag, the heavenly smells making her mouth water.

"It's New Year's Eve. Why shouldn't we have good food, good company and..."

"Good booze!" Marcus finished.

He withdrew two bottles of Dom Pérignon from one bag and from the other, two bottles of sparkling cider.

"For the lady." He smiled.

"Daddy," Simone whispered.

Seth looked up and noticed Connor for the first time.

"I'm sorry, baby. I didn't even realize your company had arrived already."

"Connor's been here for almost an hour. You guys took forever," Josette complained as she nibbled on a piece of garlic bread, which she'd retrieved from one of the dozen containers.

"Connor, this is my dad, Seth Crawford."

"Hey, youngblood," Seth said, shaking hands with Connor.

"It's nice to finally meet you, sir. Simone talks about you all the time," Connor said.

"And this is my big-headed little brother, Marcus," Simone said.

"What's up, man?" Marcus said, slapping five

with Connor before reaching over to shove Simone playfully.

"Marcus, don't hit your sister," Seth admonished.

"I didn't hit her.... I pushed her," Marcus defended.

"Oh. Well, that's okay then." Seth laughed.

"Daddy!" Simone exclaimed.

"Let's eat," Josette chimed in.

The food was carried into the dining room where place settings had already been laid out by Simone earlier that evening. The family joked and laughed all evening. Shortly before midnight, it began to snow. Josette insisted that Connor stay over in the guest room and drive home in the morning. There would be too many *New Year's nuts* on the road, as she liked to call them, taking dangerous chances in the inclement weather. She would not take no for an answer and made him call his parents to advise them of the plan. They gathered in the den, tuning in to watch the ball drop, and shortly afterward Seth led the sleepy Josette up to their bedroom. The kids continued watching television until the wee hours of the morning.

Despite the rocky start, the new year seemed to take off in the right direction. By the time the kids left to return to their respective schools, Josette had begun to believe that everything would truly work out for the best. Seth's smile had returned and she was enjoying the way everyone fussed over her, especially him. The nausea had all but subsided and she began to feel a bit more energetic. Yes, things were definitely looking up.

Chapter 18

Josette awoke with a start. She sat up in bed and glanced at the clock. It was just after two o'clock in the morning. She ran a hand through tangled hair, her heart still racing from the dream she'd had. It was a nightmare, in fact, and while she could not recall the exact details, she remembered running and calling out to Seth, who did not answer.

She turned to Seth's side of the bed to find it empty. She looked again at the clock and then toward the window. Nothing but darkness peeped around the heavy drapes. Where could he be? She climbed out of bed, wrapping her arms around her body, which felt cold and was covered with goose bumps. She padded in bare feet down the hallway. From the top of the stairs she could see a blue light coming from the den. The door was slightly ajar. She figured that Seth must have been unable to sleep and come downstairs to read so as not to disturb her. Making her way down the steps, she reached the den, but before she could open the door all the way, she caught a glimpse of Seth. His back was to her and he was typing on the computer. The blue light was from the monitor screen.

"Seth, I know you're not working at this hour," she said softly, pushing the door open and entering the room.

Seth nearly jumped out of his skin. He quickly pressed the power button, causing the computer screen to go black, and whirled around in his seat.

"I'm sorry, honey. I didn't mean to startle you," Josette said.

"It's, uh… It's okay."

Seth stood and moved toward Josette.

"What were you doing?" she asked, peering behind him at the now-darkened computer screen. "Why'd you shut the computer off like that?"

"Huh? Uh…no reason. I was just finishing up, anyway. What are you doing up?" he asked.

"I had a nightmare," Josette replied.

Suddenly, Josette felt a chill even stronger than the one that had awoken her from her sleep. She looked at Seth, who immediately looked away from her.

"Come on. Let's go back to bed," he said.

She allowed him to lead her back up the stairs. She tossed and turned for the remainder of the night, lying awake for hours and listening to his light snoring beside her. There was something wrong and, although she did not know what it was, she felt it as surely as she felt the little life growing inside of her.

They awoke late in the morning, both tired from the middle-of-the-night sleep interruption they'd experienced. Seth hurried off to work, while Josette took her time. As long as she didn't allow her stomach to remain empty for long, she could ward off the nausea, making her feel better than she had for the past few weeks. Unfortunately, when she didn't get a good night's rest, she was sluggish. She showered and dressed, taking her time.

Looking at her reflection in the mirror, she smoothed her hand over her belly. She remembered that with Simone she had not begun to show until the end of her fourth month of pregnancy, but with Marcus her stomach had begun to protrude at the start of the third month. Unable to see any visible signs of the baby now, she reminded herself that every pregnancy was different. This time she'd probably wake up one morning to find that her belly had popped out overnight.

As she headed down the stairs, the memory of Seth's strange behavior the night before came back to her suddenly. She felt herself drawn to the den. She stepped inside, peering around the room as if she'd never been inside of it before. Nothing jumped out at her. The room had been designed initially with everyone in mind, but over the years it had pretty much morphed into Seth's room. Seth's work area contained an oak desk, shelves that lined one wall and contained books for all ages, of all types. The brown, brushed-cotton sofa faced a forty-six-inch flat-panel television, which was Seth's pride and joy. In one corner of the room was a brass-and-glass rolling bar that contained bottles of liquor that had yet to be opened, as neither Josette nor Seth were much for drinking.

Her eyes were drawn back to the desk, which was relatively neat, aside from a couple of stacks of papers, a note pad, some writing utensils and an opened business-law reference manual. She walked over to the computer and pressed the power button on the monitor. Slowly, the screen faded in, blue light filling the room. She pulled out the desk chair and sat down as words appeared in front of her. Apparently, in his haste to shut down last night, Seth had only turned off the screen and not the computer itself. She realized that he had been logged on to the Internet and had been in the middle of typing an e-mail when she'd interrupted him. As the words took shape and appeared before her, the tiny hairs stood up on the back of her neck. Realizing that she was about to read words that she probably did not want to know existed, she read on anyway, compelled to find out why her sudden appearance in a room would make her husband so nervous.

Thirty minutes went by in which Josette got more than what she had bargained for. By the time she'd read the last word of every e-mail in Seth's incoming, old and sent folders, she could no longer feel anything. It was as if the blood had been sucked out of her body and nothing coursed through her veins at all. She sat in stunned silence, unable to move a muscle. Her body grew numb from remaining in the same position for so long. The telephone began ringing from somewhere in the house, but she did not stir. When her cell phone began ringing from her purse, which was still on her shoulder, she finally snapped out of the stupor she'd been in, reached inside and pulled it out. The call was from her office.

"Hello?" she whispered, unable to make her voice register any louder.

"Josette? Is that you?" Natalie asked.

"Yes…. What is it, Natalie?"

"Josette, what's wrong? Are you okay? Is it the baby?" Natalie asked, alarmed.

"I'm fine. I…" Josette trailed off, unable to find the words to finish her sentence.

"Where are you? It's almost twelve o'clock. When you called me at eight, you said you'd be in by nine-thirty or so."

"I'm at home."

"Josette, why didn't you answer the house phone? Is Seth with you?"

"No, he's at work," she said, then added, "I think," because she really wasn't sure where he was. She could not be sure of anything at the moment.

"Josette, I'm going to call Seth. You don't sound like you should be alone."

"No!" Josette screamed. "Do *not* call him."

Her sudden outburst caused Natalie to grow even more concerned.

"Look, Josette, I don't know what's going on, but I'm on my way up there. I'll be there soon, okay?"

"Yes," Josette whispered before hanging up the telephone.

Finally, the tears that had been frozen behind her eyes began to fall. She sat and cried long and hard, her body racked with emotion. She moved from the desk chair to the sofa and then to the floor, clutching the vibrantly colored throw pillow she'd pulled down with her. She buried her face in it and screamed, anguished and animalistic sounds emanating from the deepest part of her soul.

Chapter 19

"Come on, Josette. Just stop for a minute and think about what you're doing," Natalie pleaded.

Josette continued stuffing her clothing haphazardly into a duffel bag, ignoring Natalie. She stalked over to her closet and snatched several hangers with clothes on them from the pole. She didn't focus on what she was grabbing—slacks with tops that didn't match, skirts that probably would not fit over her growing belly within a few weeks. Her mind was focused on one thing, and that was getting away before Seth came home. She could not trust herself to face him just yet. She returned to the bed and roughly shoved the pile into a waiting garment bag.

"Tsk," she said, sucking her teeth with venom. "I have thought about it. I have thought about nothing else for the past two hours. Ever since I discovered that my husband...the man I'd spent the past twenty-one years with, was out on the prowl, trying to find some young, warm body to push up and into, that's all I've been able to think about," Josette spat.

When Natalie had arrived at the Crawford residence after the cryptic conversation with Josette, she'd used the spare key that Josette kept in a desk drawer at the office. Luckily, Natalie had had the foresight to grab it, since Josette had not answered the door when she'd knocked repeatedly. Natalie had found her friend and colleague curled up on the floor beside the sofa in the den with tears streaming down her face and snot bubbling out of her nose. It had taken quite some time for her to get Josette to calm down and to tell her what was wrong. When she finally had, Natalie, too, had been utterly speechless. She could not believe that Josette had read what she'd claimed to have read in Seth's e-mails, nor could she fathom that Seth would have written those words in the first place. However, Josette pointed to the computer screen and the proof was right there, in black and white.

It seemed that Seth had developed a friendship with a woman. Cutie215 was her screen name and, according to the dates of the e-mails, they had been corresponding off and on since last summer. Many of their messages where harmless banter about a variety of things, including inquiries about work, family and things like that. However, as time progressed, some of them became quite explicit. Seth had been expressing sexual desires to this woman, talking to her about the things he liked to do and the way he liked to do them, and Miss Cutie wrote extensively about her ability to satisfy any or all of those fantasies.

"But, Josette, twenty-one years... Can you really just throw away all of that? All these years together... Don't you believe that you guys have a life that's worth preserving?" Natalie asked.

Natalie knew that Josette was hurting, but she wanted her friend to think about the fact that this was her husband—not just some guy she'd been dating. The two of them had been together for a long time and, from everything she had ever observed, they loved one another.

"He's the one who threw it away. The moment his fingertips caressed that keyboard as he spelled out his fantasies and secret desires with a woman he didn't know...a woman who wasn't me...he threw it away. I'm just picking up on his cue, following his lead if you will."

Natalie sighed, knowing that there was no way she would get through to Josette right now. She couldn't blame her for being angry. Lord knows she would probably kill Todd if he did something like that. But she and Todd had only been married for seven years. That was a mere sneeze when you compared it to Josette and Seth. Besides, Seth and Josette were an older couple. One would think that at that point in life, folks would be immune to such things as infidelity and mistrust. The idea that these types of issues could face a couple after such a long time together shook Natalie's faith in marriage in general, and her own in particular, to the core.

"Josette, you are right. He was wrong, dead wrong, and I'm not going to pretend to know how you feel right now. But can you really condemn a man for his thoughts and words? I mean, he hasn't actually done anything."

"Not yet, Natalie," Josette exclaimed, whirling around from her dresser drawers. In her hands was a pile of undergarments, which she tossed into an overnight bag. "It's just a matter of time. If Miss Cutie upped the ante and tried to set up a face-to-face, he'd probably be all over it."

"You don't know that," Natalie said, shaking her head emphatically.

Josette stared out into space for a moment, her mind foggy as images of Seth passed before her memory.

"I do. You don't know Seth the way I do. You haven't seen the new spring in his step, the light in his eyes. I noticed it before, but it didn't really stand out until now. Ever since he's been dealing with her, I guess, it's like he's back to being that old Seth, the one I met back in college. Stupid,

stupid me.... I thought I was the cause of all that happiness."

Josette sank down on the bed next to her bags, looking defeated and heartbroken.

"He's happy, except it has nothing to do with me," she added.

Natalie sat beside her and rubbed her back, not knowing what to say. She felt completely inept and way out of her league. Josette was over ten years her senior and had always seemed to have it going on. Josette was the kind of woman whom Natalie could look up to, a mentor in many respects. To watch her going through this hurt, Natalie felt as if she were going through it in a way. It also made her feel as if there were no hope for the sanctity of love and marriage. Try as she might, she could not completely shake the feeling of doom that was spreading over her, despite trying to remain the voice of optimism for Josette's sake.

"I really thought that we would be together forever. I know things haven't been hot and heavy between us for years, but I thought that we were regaining some of that passion. I mean, what about our plans? We were planning to spend our twenty-first wedding anniversary abroad. What a joke. How could he do this to me?" Josette asked.

"I don't know, sweetie," Natalie said, continuing to rub her back. "You need some time," she said after a while. "You need a little bit of time to think about everything and sort it all out. I just don't think you should make any rash decisions right now. Why don't you come over to my place and spend the night, the weekend, or whatever. Give yourself some time to digest this and then, when you're calmer, maybe you can talk to Seth."

"I don't want to talk to him," Josette said, a fresh round of tears running down her puffy face.

"Josette, you're going to have to talk to him sooner or later. What about the kids…the baby?"

Josette rubbed her belly and shook her head at the same time. Her baby didn't deserve to come into the world amid confusion and betrayal, but that was exactly what was happening. Josette stood up and continued gathering some of her belongings. She had no intentions of being there when Seth returned home. She didn't feel strong enough to deal with him right now. While she had not developed a solid plan, she knew enough to know that she had to leave.

After considering the option of staying at a hotel, she realized that she did not want to be alone. In all the years of her marriage, she had never stayed away from Seth in anger. Despite the fact that they'd had disagreements over the years, there had never been any problem that had resulted in one of them packing a bag to live separately from the other. Up to this point, there had never been a need for it. Going to a hotel would make that a stark reality, and she was not quite prepared for that. She decided to take Natalie up on her offer until she could figure out what she was going to do. Her note to Seth was short and to the point. She left it on top of the keyboard of his beloved computer, left her car in the driveway and climbed into the passenger seat of Natalie's car without looking back.

Chapter 20

By nightfall, Seth had called Josette's cell phone so many times that the battery had finally died. She'd refused to answer the phone nor did she listen to the more than a dozen messages that he'd left in the voice mail. Eventually, he'd tracked down Natalie's home number and began calling her house. After securing Josette in their spare bedroom, Natalie had filled her husband, Todd, in on the circumstances. When Seth called, it was Todd who answered the telephone and spoke to him. He assured Seth that Josette was okay and that he and Natalie would take care of her. He told him that Josette refused to talk to him right now, but from one man to another, he understood Seth's agony and counseled him to keep trying to get through to his wife.

Todd and Seth had only met on a couple of occasions, but to Todd, Seth seemed like a good brother. He was surprised that he had gotten himself into this predicament, but he was not about to judge the man. They talked briefly, during which Seth sounded as if he were about to break down. He thanked Todd for looking after Josette, asked him to call him if she began feeling ill or anything and then hung up. Todd's heart went out to the man.

Two days later, Josette felt as if she had cried all the tears she could possibly cry. She grew tired of moping around Natalie's home and looking and feeling like crap. Natalie had been a true friend; they'd commuted back and forth to the office together and she'd held her hand through the tears and the outbursts. Sitting up with Josette late into the night, Natalie had gotten her through the hysterics and helped her to regain control over the insanity that descended when a woman felt violated.

Seth had sent her a bouquet of roses and a long letter in which he promised that he had never been unfaithful to her...had never considered being unfaithful to her. He begged her to come home, which, on the third day, she did.

Josette entered their home that evening, her

heart heavy, but her mind purposeful. She had invested too much into her marriage and into building a life with Seth to watch it go up in smoke without at least a conversation. She needed to talk to her husband, and without knowing whether they would be able to salvage what they had, she knew that they owed one another at least a chance to talk.

Seth was sitting alone at the counter in the kitchen. Before him was a half-eaten deli sandwich and an unopened copy of the *New York Times* newspaper. He looked up when she entered, his ashen face appearing as if he was two days overdue for a shave. A hesitant smile appeared on his lips, freezing there. He looked down at the bags in Josette's hands, jumping up from the stool.

"Here, let me take those," he said, pointing to the bags.

Josette handed them over to him, removed her coat and walked away from the kitchen. She went into the living room, switched on a lamp and sat down on the butter-yellow leather sofa. Seth entered the room slowly, not knowing what to say to her. Quietly, he took a seat in a brown over-stuffed armchair across from her and waited anxiously.

Josette looked around the room, remembering how much pleasure she had derived from decorating it. She'd chosen to use an autumn theme in the room—shades of brown and orange were dominant while the yellow sofa gave it a burst of brightness. This room was the showroom—the room company was invited into when they came by. Otherwise, it remained unoccupied for the most part. Sitting in there with Seth under the circumstances they now found themselves in, she felt as though they were on neutral ground.

"Did you remember to take Lady to the vet yesterday? I forgot about her appointment," Josette asked at length.

"I rescheduled the appointment for next Tuesday. Dr. Rodman had an emergency. I'll take her in next week," Seth answered.

Silence ensued, each of them knowing that a discussion was forthcoming, but both unsure as to where to begin.

"Seth," Josette said finally.

She took a deep breath.

"Baby, I'm so sorry," Seth interrupted.

"Just wait," Josette commanded, halting him. "I need to try to understand what happened between us. I need for you to explain to me...how we got here."

"Josette, baby, I want to explain. I want you to understand. I...I was stupid. Plain and simple, I was just stupid. But you've got to know that I never, ever for one minute meant to hurt you."

"But you did, Seth.... You did."

"I know that, and if I could take it back, I would in an instant. I don't know what I was thinking…what I was looking for. It was all talk, Josette. That's it…. Nothing more than talk, I swear to you. I never intended to do anything with her."

"Who is she?"

"She's a junior partner at Bradley, Roth. They're a Philadelphia-based law firm with whom we've shared some business over the years."

"So you've worked with her?"

"Not directly. She's mostly tax and finance…not closely related to what I do. We met last year when she attended a deposition being held at our offices. Honestly, Josette, it was a professional friendship, at first."

"And then?" Josette said, cringing.

"I don't know how things changed. I just found her easy to talk to about some of the things on my mind," he admitted.

He hung his head shamefully, knowing how that must have sounded to his wife.

"Why couldn't you talk to me?" Josette asked.

That was the question that had been foremost on her mind for the past three days. At one time, she and Seth had been able to talk through the night, until the sun came up. Wrapped in one another's arms, they would talk about their dreams, their fears, their triumphs and their shortcomings. There was nothing that they had not shared with one another, unafraid to bear their naked souls before each other. When that had changed, she had no clue.

"I don't know why, Josette. It just seemed like over the years, we grew further and further apart. You became so involved in other things—"

"Involved in other things? What the hell are you talking about, Seth?" Josette said, becoming angry. "This house, this family has been my number-one priority…always."

"I'm not blaming you, Josette. I had no business doing what I did. I'm just trying to make some sense of things. You and I were best friends, but over the years…things changed. You became this awesome mother, and I was so proud of you. My life with you was a dream come true. I never knew that I could love someone so much, and you made me feel loved and supported."

"So why, Seth?"

"I don't know. Maybe… Maybe it was because I was missing you," Seth said, his voice low.

Josette looked at Seth, confused by his words to the point that she could not fathom that he had said them.

"What did you say?" she asked.

"I missed you. I missed my wife. Every night I went to sleep next to you, and every morning I woke up beside you. We talked periodically throughout the day…about this and that, the kids, the bills, things that needed to be done. But, Josie," he said, calling her the pet name that he used to call her during their first few years of marriage.

His voice broke and he buried his face in his

hands. He felt ashamed of himself. A big-time lawyer, an older and established man falling to pieces because he felt alone.

"Josie, I missed you so much. I felt like you were there for everyone else...everyone except me," he admitted, looking his wife in the eyes.

Despite the sincerity she saw in his face and the undeniable truth that rang in his words, Josette was miles away from understanding him.

"Are you putting this on me, Seth? Are you going to sit here and say you began a relationship with another woman because of something you perceived that I did to you...or didn't do for you?" she asked incredulously.

"It wasn't a relationship, Josette. Don't make it out to be more than what it was. She was nothing.... She is nothing to me, and no, I'm not trying to blame you for this. I'm just telling you how I feel."

Josette shook her head vehemently, her hair swinging from side to side.

"No, no...no, Seth. This is not about me. This is about you. You can sit here and sugarcoat things all you want to, but what you have with her—"

"Had, Josette. Had. I haven't communicated with her since the day you left."

"Forgive me if I don't believe that, Seth, but whatever. Any time you sit down with someone who is not your wife and share the type of intimacies that you and she shared... It does not have to be physical, Seth. It's still a relationship."

Seth sat quietly, unwilling to argue semantics with Josette because whether he agreed with her or not, he knew that it would not make one bit of a difference to their situation. Josette stood up and walked across the room. She stood near the living room's bay window, looking out at the darkness. The sprawling lawn, the lush, twenty-foot flowering crabapple tree with its branches now naked and the lonely streetlight about three houses down. The normalcy of these things seemed so contradictory to what was going on behind the glass, within her heart.

"Seth," she said at last. "I'm not going to pretend to understand why you felt like you couldn't come to me. I know that things have changed between us and I'll admit, I've been afraid for us…. Afraid for myself. These past few months have been strange to me as I've attempted to get to know myself again. I thought that I was working at that, and I believed that things were getting better between us."

"They were. I can't tell you how I was feeling lately. I enjoyed seeing you doing things again…singing in the choir, dancing. I mean, sure, I was worried at first that these would just add to the list of things that kept you away from me, but I realized that that was not the case. I enjoyed making love to you again…feeling like you wanted me as much as you did when we were younger, but—"

"But you couldn't resist talking to your friend?"

"No. I had stopped communicating with her...until—"

Slowly, understanding spread across Josette's face.

"Until the baby," she finished for him.

Seth didn't answer. There was no need for him to answer because the truth was sitting right there in between them. He had not wanted this baby. He had not pretended to be happy about it in the least. However, for Josette, this silent admission was like a knife in her heart, for as much as she had been taken by surprise by the pregnancy, she had not really understood how opposed to it Seth had been. Now this realization left a taste in her mouth so bitter that she could not swallow it.

"I'm sorry, Josette," Seth said again.

And he was. He was sorry that he had not been able to just accept the surprise pregnancy the way she had. He was still not able to do so. He was sorry that he had not been able just to come right out and tell her how he felt, how he had been feeling for a long time. What was more, he was sorry that he had hurt her. He wanted to reach out to her now and touch her. He wanted to hold her in his arms and confess the sins of his thoughts, the betrayal of his emotions. He ached just to be able to feel her heartbeat against his and know that somehow things would work themselves out. He would have given anything for that to happen, but as he looked at her stoic face, he knew that they were a long way away from that point.

"I need to lie down," she said.

Josette pulled herself away from the window and walked out of the room. She went up the stairs, deliberately, one at a time and entered their bedroom. She did not turn on the lights, nor did she remove her clothing. She lay across the bed and closed her eyes, overcome by fatigue both physically and mentally. Sleep descended on her almost immediately, and she gratefully accepted it.

Seth climbed the stairs several times that night. The first time he stood in the doorway and by the light shed from the glow of the hallway fixture, he watched her sleep. The second time, he crept into the room and pulled a blanket up over her sleeping frame. The third time, several hours later, he lay on the bed beside her, inhaled her sweet smell and fell asleep, grateful that physically at least his wife was back at home. He told himself that everything else would come in time.

The next few days in the Crawford home were as quiet as an elementary-school gymnasium in the summertime. There was no laughter, no chatter, not even the sound of quiet studies or contemplation. Seth moved about feeling like an outsider in his own home. He tried to engage Josette in conversation on more than one occasion, commenting on silly, benign matters in the hope that slowly he would be able to ease her back into some form of dialogue. However, his inquiries and comments were met with one, two at best, word answers and

not much else. For her part, Josette did not intentionally attempt to shut Seth out. She was just trying
hard to make sense of things, and she felt as though
she could not do that for herself and for him at the
same time. The anger she'd felt had long since dissipated, and in its place was a profound sense of disappointment.

She went to work each morning, determined not
to allow her own messy affairs to interfere with the
assistance that other women and their families
needed from her agency. Natalie pitched in
overtime, taking up the slack whenever Josette
faltered. Without speaking, the women shared an
almost telepathic connection, and Natalie knew
when Josette needed time alone, or, alternatively, a
box of tissues and a shoulder to cry on. She made
sure that Josette ate a hearty breakfast and a nour-
ishing lunch each day, often bringing in leftovers
from the dinner she'd prepared the night before.
Josette's gratitude for her friend's kindness and consideration showed in her eyes and did not need to
be spoken.

When they did talk, Natalie expressed admira-
tion at the way Josette was handling things. She
fully supported her decision to go home and to stay
there, despite knowing that it had been a difficult
one for her to come to. As much as she despised
what Seth had done, Natalie still believed that he
was a good man who loved his wife and had not
intentionally hurt her. She held on to that belief and

to the belief that Seth and Josette would be able to get past this indiscretion. She said a prayer for them each and every night, adding in a prayer for her own marriage, as well.

A week after Josette's return home, Seth came home early from work. He went directly into the kitchen, laden with packages and set about creating a masterpiece for dinner.

By the time Josette arrived, the aroma of his efforts greeted her as she turned the key in the lock of the front door. She peered into the dining room first, noting that he had laid out an elegant table setting for two. She followed the delicious scents to the kitchen, where her eyes were met by complete and utter chaos, and her husband.

Covered from head to toe in flour and various food stains, his shirtsleeves rolled up and his reading glasses sitting crookedly on his face, Seth smiled weakly at her.

"Hi, babe.... Uh, dinner's just about ready," he said.

If he hadn't looked so pathetic, it would have been easy for Josette to laugh in his face and march upstairs unmoved. However, the fact was, the food smelled good, and it was obvious that he had gone through a lot of trouble to please her. She nodded her head.

"All right. Call me when it's ready," she said.

Thirty minutes went by before Seth had managed to rinse the dishes and load them into the dishwasher, scrub the spills from the countertops, the stove and himself, mop the flour-covered kitchen floor and set dinner on the table. Josette joined him in the dining room, where he pulled out her seat for her, lit the two tapered candles and sat down across the table from her. He'd done an excellent job at re-creating Josette's recipe for a three-cheese baked manicotti and a balsamic salad with mixed greens, tomatoes and cheese. She dug in heartily, the food's enticing display luring her appetite.

"Are you going into the office tomorrow morning before your doctor's appointment?" Seth asked.

Josette looked up at him, surprised that he had remembered she was scheduled for the second sonogram with Dr. Tucker tomorrow at eleven o'clock.

"I was planning to work from here and then catch the ten-something train into the city," she answered.

"I'll drive you," he said.

The meaning behind his words, although unspoken, was clear to both of them. She regarded him for a moment, seeing the man she'd fallen in love with seated across from her instead of the stranger she had been living with since the day she'd read his secret thoughts. Her faint smile was enough to give him hope. They enjoyed the rest of dinner in comfortable silence. That night, as they lay in bed, he found the courage to move closer to

her despite his fear that she would turn him away.
He wrapped his arms around her and she settled
against him, falling asleep.

Chapter 21

The next morning, as Josette lay on the examining table awaiting Dr. Tucker's arrival into the room, she began to feel strange. Anxiety filled her chest cavity, making it difficult for her to breathe. She looked at Seth, who read the tension in her eyes and immediately jumped up from his seat, discarding the magazine he had been leafing through, and grabbed her hand.

"What is it, Josette?" he asked.

"I don't know. Something's wrong, Seth. I just know it," she said.

"Shh, babe. Everything is fine. I'm sure of it. Don't worry. Dr. Tucker will come in in just a minute and you'll see," he said.

Right on cue, Dr. Tucker entered the room.

"Well, if it isn't my favorite parents-to-be. How are you, Seth?" Dr. Tucker said, extending a hand.

"Good, Doctor. Can't complain."

"That's good to hear. And how's Mama Bear over there?" Dr. Tucker asked, smiling in Josette's direction. "I bet she's giving you a run for the money these days, heh?"

"Nah, she's not bad at all. Not bad at all," Seth defended.

"I get it…. You've got to go home with her, right?" Dr. Tucker laughed conspiratorially.

He slid on a pair of plastic gloves and walked over to Josette. The technician had set up the sonogram machine and placed a stool near the side of the examining table where Josette lay waiting.

"Hey, Dr. Tucker," she said.

"What's wrong, pretty lady? You don't sound like the bubbly dynamo I've come to know and love," Dr. Tucker commented.

"I don't know, Doc. Guess I'm getting a little too old for this business." Josette laughed.

"Nonsense. You are just as spry as when we cooked up that little girl of yours. Now, what's say we take a peek at your new baby and see what's happening in there?"

Josette nodded her head. She was anxious to see the baby and to know that everything was all right. She hadn't given any thought to whether it was a girl or a boy, nor did she care. All she wanted to do was find out that the baby was healthy and growing the way it should be. Anything else they found out today would pale in comparison to that knowledge.

Dr. Tucker squeezed a silver dollar coin–size amount of the clear gel onto her abdomen. He apologized for the coldness and then began the examination by pressing the camera against her stomach. He moved it around slowly, starting at the far left side and gliding across to the right. He moved back to the center and upward, going ever so slowly, then returning to the center of her belly, circling around her navel and then downward to the top of her pubic region. This went on for about four or five minutes, during which time Dr. Tucker said nothing and Josette grew increasingly agitated.

Dr. Tucker turned the machine off. He pulled his stethoscope from around his neck, inserted the earpieces into his ears and pressed the scope against Josette's belly. He moved it around slowly for several minutes, his face unreadable. Finally, he performed an internal examination, pressing against her cervix several times. Then, he removed his gloves and took a seat on the stool. Josette sat up and Seth immediately went to her side.

"Mr. and Mrs. Crawford, I'm very sorry," he began.

Josette shut her eyes, wishing she could do the same for her ears. She was unwilling to hear what Dr. Tucker was about to say to them. Seth put his arm around Josette's shoulder, pulling her closer to him.

"The baby has no detectable fetal heart rate," Dr. Tucker said gravely.

"What does that mean?" Seth asked.

Josette tried to block out their conversation, knowing full well what it meant.

"Well, when an egg is fertilized by sperm, it is supposed to travel through the fallopian tube to the uterus, where it should implant itself to the walls of the uterus and grow there. In this case, the egg has attached to an area outside of the uterus…in the fallopian tube. Unfortunately, this area is incapable of sustaining a growing fetus—there is just not enough room. As a result, the fetus cannot be brought to full term."

Seth closed his eyes for a moment, the reality of what the doctor was telling them finally sinking in. He felt Josette begin to shiver and he clutched his arm around her more tightly.

"How did this happen? I mean, aren't the odds against something like this pretty great?" Seth wanted to know.

"There is no exact way to determine what happens in each case and yes, you are accurate that this is not something that we see very often. What I suspect in Josette's case is that there may have been some scar tissue which developed after the surgery on her ovary which may have caused this."

Josette silently wished that Seth would just stop

asking questions and that both he and Dr. Tucker would stop talking. Their voices seemed so loud, reverberating in her ears, and all she wanted was silence for just a moment.

"What's going to happen now?" Seth asked.

"Well, we will have to remove the fetus," Dr. Tucker replied.

"You're going to have to operate?"

"Yes, that is the best course of action. You see, there is sometimes the option of treating the condition medically, however, that is most effective when the fetus has only been growing for three or four weeks. Even then, there is no guarantee and we would have to run tests in a few weeks to make sure that the medicine effectively aborted the fetus. In this case, I think that the pregnancy has progressed further than that and based on my examination, I think that we cannot wait any longer," Dr. Tucker said, looking Seth directly in the eye. "Mr. and Mrs. Crawford, there is a possibility that the enlarged fetus could cause the fallopian tube to burst, resulting in a life-threatening condition."

Tears streamed down Josette's crestfallen face. Dr. Tucker left the room, giving the couple time alone to grieve. He had his receptionist make the necessary arrangements at Mount Sinai Hospital so that they would be prepared for Josette's arrival that afternoon. He gave orders that the couple be allowed to remain in the examination room for as long as they needed to and also that all of his appointments after three o'clock be canceled and re-scheduled for tomorrow.

Seth held Josette's shaking body in his arms, rocking her softly as she cried. His own tears were frozen in his eyes, making liquid pools form that blurred his vision. He held his body erect, allowing himself not a moment of weakness as he stood as her rock. Eventually, she allowed him to pull her from the table. He dressed her as if she were a baby, his baby, and he led her from the room, her head down, her tear-streaked face buried in his shoulder. He put her in the passenger seat of the car, and she shrank against the window. He drove the ten minutes to the hospital in silence, save for the sounds of afternoon traffic, which surrounded their vehicle.

Josette was admitted immediately, placed in a wheelchair and taken upstairs to a private room on the surgical floor. Seth remained downstairs in admissions, filling out the necessary paperwork. When he arrived in her room, Josette was already in a hospital gown, with an intravenous needle and tube inserted into her left arm, liquids being fed into her through a tube, and she was lying on the bed, a thin white blanket pulled up to her neck. Her eyes were closed, but he could tell that she was awake from the moisture that slid down her cheeks. He pulled up a chair next to her and sat, taking her hand in his.

While Josette was in the operating room, Seth

went downstairs to make the necessary calls. He called her parents first, knowing that her mother would be expecting to receive her nightly call from Josette and would become worried if she didn't hear from her. After that conversation, he felt devoid of the energy to talk to anyone else, but he knew that he had to. Her mother's anguish over her daughter's pain came through the lines loud and clear, and she dropped the phone, bursting into a chorus of *aye dios mios* and various other Spanish phrases. Josette's father picked up the phone, causing Seth to have to repeat the tragic news. After commanding Seth to call them back after the procedure to let them know how Josette was doing, Benjamin Medwala hung up to see after his wife.

The next call Seth made was to Natalie. She had probably been expecting Josette in the office that afternoon. Once he told her what the situation was, surprisingly Natalie offered her concern for him.

"How are you doing, Seth?" she asked.

"Me?" he replied, surprised by the question.

"Yeah. I know this can't be easy for you."

"I'm fine.... I'm fine," he insisted, although he felt as though his world had fallen apart.

He knew that Josette had undoubtedly told Natalie about his reaction to the baby. She had, after all, stayed in Natalie's home during their brief separation. He could only imagine what Natalie must have thought of him, but for her to show concern for his well-being now truly meant a lot to him.

"Well, if there is anything I can do…for either of you, Seth, please call me. Day or night, okay?" she said.

"Thank you, Natalie," was all he could manage to say.

He hung up the phone, deciding that any other calls would have to wait. Seth slumped down into an olive-green, hard plastic chair, one in a row of seven that lined the back wall of the waiting room. He'd intended to make the necessary phone calls and then return immediately to the surgical ward so that he would be there when Josette was wheeled out of the operating room. However, doubting that his legs could carry him back down the brightly lit corridor, through the double set of swinging doors, into the elevator and back out onto the third floor, he remained where he was for a while. His gut wrenched, alternating between a tightening sensation as if his intestines were being squeezed with a vise grip, and a slack, weightless feeling as if he were a liquid surrounded by and immersed in liquids. The air he sucked into his greedy lungs tasted stale. Nothing made sense but at the same time his mind screamed for clarity. He realized, seated on that hard chair, with no clear definition of time or day, that his love for Josette was the only thing that had rhyme or reason in his whole world. She was everything to him and the fact was he had lost sight of that recently, allowing him to put himself before his wife—something he had not done since the day he'd met her.

The question he asked himself now was when he'd stopped considering the *we* and grown concerned solely about the *I*. Had he not done so, he would have figured out a way to address their common needs and concerns, as opposed to seeking an outlet for what ailed him alone. Seth ground his teeth together, a useless attempt to suppress anger at his selfish and potentially self-destructive behavior. He sprang from the chair suddenly, the absurd thought that if something went wrong as Dr. Tucker had posed as a possibility and Josette did not make it off that table, she would never know how sorry he was for hurting her. He raced down the hallway, ignoring the threatening looks from the hospital personnel whom he whipped past. He burst from the elevator onto the surgical floor and was reaching out to push open the door that would lead to the outer chamber of the operating rooms, when it opened on its own. Dr. Tucker emerged, halting Seth in his tracks.

"Dr. Tucker, how is she? Is she okay?" Seth demanded breathlessly.

"Yes, Mr. Crawford, your wife is doing just fine. I was just coming out to get you. She's being prepared to go into the recovery room, but she demanded that I come and get you."

Dr. Tucker led Seth back through the doors, where a nurse helped him into a paper gown and mask while Dr. Tucker talked.

"Now, I want you to know that there was quite a bit of bleeding. We used a laparoscope, which allowed for a small incision, which should heal nicely. The tube was seriously damaged, which confirms my suspicions that we caught this just in time."

"Thank you, Dr. Tucker," Seth said, preparing to enter the room.

"There is one more thing. As I told you, the damage was severe. We had to go ahead and tie off Josette's tubes. I'm sorry, Mr. Crawford, but she will never conceive any more children."

Seth nodded slowly, the finality of the doctor's words pressing against his mind. However, he could not allow himself to dwell on that right now. He knew that he needed to be strong and support Josette. His own feelings would have to wait.

"Seth?" Josette called weakly.

Seth looked down at Josette, fresh tears spilling from her eyes as they met his. He knelt over her, kissing her forehead tenderly while he wiped her cheeks with his hand.

"I'm here, babe. Right here. Dr. Tucker says you did just fine. Everything's okay," he soothed.

"Our baby, Seth… Our baby," she moaned.

"Shh, I know…. I know…. It's okay, Josette. It's going to be all right. I promise you. I'm going to take you home and take care of you. Shh, don't cry, babe…. I'm right here," Seth said.

Seth stayed by Josette's side all night, at first

seated in a chair by her bed and holding her hand, then later transferring onto the tiny twin mattress with her. The small, neutral-colored hospital room felt cold and sterile, lacking the fetal-like warmth of their home. He wished that he could take her there, knowing that while that would not completely heal her broken heart, it would be a step in the right direction. Josette's sleep was fitful that night. She alternated between sleeping, crying out and moaning. Each time, Seth was roused from his own restless slumber. He pulled her closer to him, rubbing her wherever he could reach and kissing her face, which was often wet with tears.

For each of them, that night was the longest night of their respective lives and when morning came, despair carried them into the new day and followed them home. Try as he might, Seth could do nothing to erase the past and Josette resisted his efforts to move them toward a brighter future.

Chapter 22

Seth pulled the car to a stop along the yellow-lined curb at John F. Kennedy Airport's departing flights. Popping the trunk, he got out of the car and rounded the vehicle. At the same time, Josette climbed out of the passenger side. They met at the back of the car. Seth pulled the garment bag out of the trunk and handed it to Josette. Next he retrieved the large suitcase on wheels, carrying it to the sidewalk. He closed the trunk, stuffed his hands into his jeans pockets and looked at his wife wordlessly.

"Well, I guess that's it. I'd better get checked in," she said.

She looked at Seth and then looked away. It was too difficult to maintain eye contact with him.

"I guess," he replied.

Neither of them made a move. The silence between them was deafening in contrast to the noisy airport sounds that were carried all around them.

"Josette—"

"Don't, Seth. Please," she said, cutting him off.

There was nothing that Seth could say to her right now that would make much difference in her tortured mind. They had already said everything that was in their hearts and minds to say, even the most hurtful things. Ironically, the day after they'd lost the baby had been the best day of the past week between them. Seth had taken Josette home and, true to his word, had taken care of everything. He'd put her to bed, made her a cup of broth and sat by her side while she'd sipped it. He'd wanted to talk, but she had not felt like it at the time. When she'd said that she was tired, he'd climbed into bed beside her and held her as she'd slept.

Later that night, Seth had fielded phone calls from family and friends, assuring them that Josette was doing just fine and asking them to give her a few days of recovery before she'd feel up to conversing. He made a light dinner for them—grilled salmon and mixed greens—which he fed Josette himself at her place in their bed. He lit a fire in the fireplace in their bedroom. With only the glow

from the embers for light, he filled a small pan
with soap and warm water and he sponged Josette's
extremities lovingly. With tenderness that came
after years of knowing and loving his mate, Seth
glided the sponge ever so slowly over her arms, up
and down the length of her legs. He refilled his pan
twice, making sure that the water remained warm
while he left no spot untouched. He sponged the
place beneath the softness of her full breasts, one
at a time. As he moved around her neck, he titled
her head back and she closed her eyes. There was
no doubt that this man, this mate of hers for the past
two decades, loved every inch of her body. That
love burned in his fingertips as he touched her, it
shone in his eyes as he watched her and it poured
from his lips as he whispered reassurances to her.
She soaked it in as completely as the sponge satu-
rated the soapy water with which he cleansed her
body in an effort to mollify her womb.

Josette, in her heartbroken state, allowed herself
to be babied by him for the first day or so without
protest. As the week progressed, she began to feel
more like herself again, and slowly she began to
grow uncomfortable under Seth's ever-present and
watchful hands. The chasm that had developed
between them resurfaced, this time with a vengeance. The more that Josette withdrew, the harder
Seth tried to get close to her, until finally the fragile
peace that had been forged shattered into a ines-
timable number of tiny pieces. She shouted and he

grunted. She screamed and he seethed. She blamed and so did he.

"You want me to believe that you understand what I am feeling and that you are feeling the same thing, Seth, when you and I both know that that is not the case," she screeched.

"What the hell is that supposed to mean?" Seth fired back. "Oh, because I'm a man, I can't possibly understand what it feels like to lose a child?"

"No, it's because you never wanted this baby in the first damned place that you can't understand!" she exploded.

All the rage that she had been feeling over the unfairness of the loss of this child, coupled with the betrayal she felt over Seth's extramarital relationship, bubbled over the surface, and she lost her composure.

They were standing in the kitchen, Seth near the coffee machine pouring fresh coffee grounds into the basket and Josette standing in front of the refrigerator searching for jam for the bagel she was about to toast in the toaster oven. Seth froze in midmotion, the sharpness of Josette's words cutting into his flesh with precision. He looked at the can of coffee grounds in his hand, feeling his fingers tremble around it. His own anger ignited and before he could stop himself, he hurled the coffee across the room. It slammed against the steel-framed clock that hung above the sink, shattering the glass and sending parts of the clock careening across the kitchen. The ticking was silenced immediately.

"How could you say that to me?" he said through clenched teeth, his voice surprisingly low.

"Isn't it the truth?"

"Just because I was having a hard time accepting the situation does not mean that I'm not hurting. It was my baby, too, Josette, or did you forget that?"

"Please, Seth. Spare me the poor-daddy routine. You didn't want the baby and now there is no baby. Don't act like that is the worst thing in the world to you because I know better," Josette said, slamming the refrigerator door.

"Josette, why are you doing this? Why are you trying to blame me for this?" Seth asked.

"I'm not blaming you, Seth, but you know what… Sometimes what you put out there comes back on you," Josette said.

She knew that she was going too far, but it was almost as though she had lost control of herself and her mouth. All the thoughts she had been having just poured from her lips without censorship and not only did she not have the ability to stop it, she did not want to. She was hurting and she wanted Seth to hurt as badly as she was.

"Josette, I'm not going to argue with you. I know that you're upset right now, and I'm sure that's why you're attacking me like this—"

"I'm, as you put it, *attacking you*, Seth, because

in one fell swoop I've had my heart, my faith and my trust snatched from beneath me. You have no idea what that feels like, and I wish you wouldn't pretend to know."

"What do you want me to do, Josette? Huh? Tell me. What can I do to make this all right for you? Because I will do it. Whatever you ask me to do, I will do it."

Seth leaned against the counter, his hands up in the air in a gesture of surrender. His face looked haggard, and Josette could clearly see that there was pain in his eyes, but she could not feel anything past her own.

"I don't know if there is anything you can do, Seth. You hurt me so badly, and I really don't know if I can get over it."

"But you came home," he said softly. "I thought that we were going to try to get through this."

Josette sighed. She had, in fact, come home, believing that it was the right thing to do. After learning of Seth's betrayal and staying away for a few days, at home with Seth she had hoped to understand what had brought them to that place. Then the baby had happened, and now it seemed as though she was even further away from the mental reconciliation she was looking for.

"I...I need some time, Seth. I think I'm going to go out and see my parents for a while," she said.

"To California?" he asked incredulously.

"Yes. I'm going to take a few days...maybe a

couple of weeks and just try to get my head straight," Josette said, making the decision at the same time that the words were coming out of her mouth.

"What are you saying to me, Josette? Are you leaving me?" Seth asked.

Josette could not answer Seth's question. She looked at him for a moment and then turned away.

"Josette, no matter what you may believe, I love you. I have loved you for more than twenty years and I'm sorry, but that shit is just not going to go away, even if that's what you want. I'm sorry I hurt you, and I make no excuses for that. I should never have talked to or confided in another woman. I know that now. But Josette, trust me, I was not looking to replace you with her. I know that I could never find a woman like you, and I wouldn't try."

Tears had slid down Josette's cheeks as she'd wanted to believe her husband but her own disappointment in him had prevented her from doing so. She had not turned around, but had simply walked out of the kitchen and into the den to make plans for her trip. Two days later, Seth drove her to the airport, hoping along the way that something would happen to change her mind. By the time they arrived at the airport, he was praying for everything from a storm to a governmental coup that would prevent her from getting on that plane. No such luck.

"You'll call me when you get there," Seth said

now as he stood watching his wife leave him for what could potentially be forever.

"Yes," Josette said.

She looked at her husband again, seeing for the first time his age, but also seeing his heart lying prostrate on his sleeve. She searched for something to say that would take some of his heartache away, but before she could speak, a traffic cop pulled up beside them, cautioning Seth to move his vehicle immediately.

"Have a safe flight, Josette," he said.

He leaned forward, rubbing his lips quickly across hers, before returning swiftly to the car and getting in. He pulled off and out into the slow stream of departing traffic as Josette watched in agony. She picked up her bags and headed for the curbside check-in. By the time she'd made it through the long but rapidly moving line, been searched by security from the top of her head to soles of her sneakers and was waiting at her flight's gate, salty tears had caused her eyes to swell.

Chapter 23

The Medwala household was one of constant laughter. They held an open-door policy—meaning that anyone and everyone was invited in at any time and for any reason. Their friends and neighbors dropped in all day long and often into the late evening hours. Lourdes Velazquez Medwala kept a pot of her strong black coffee warm, and a freshly baked cake or pie was always at the ready. Retiring from the post office had been something her husband had wanted for her more than she'd wanted for herself, and ever since she'd licked her last stamp four years ago, she'd worked hard to ward off any signs of slowing down, relaxation and solitude—she believed those to be signs of aging.

Benjamin Medwala had also retired from his job as a dietitian in a local hospice. Benjamin, a tall, handsome man with skin like black velvet, hair like silk and the wide-open face of a proud Native American chief, was giddy with joy over having the freedom to do as much or as little as he wanted to do with his days. He alternated between fishing with his good friend, fellow former hospital worker, George Martinez, hunting fowl with his brother, Eugene, or working on one of his many un-completed building projects in the garage of his home.

The house was a small, Spanish-styled bunga-low, with a white stucco exterior adorned by tur-quoise shutters. Flower-patterned lawn furniture sat on the patio out back, facing half an acre of landscaped property whose design gave the im-pression of a siesta waiting to happen. Lourdes loved vibrant colors and decorative symbols of her Mexican heritage. So while their residence was one of the more colorful ones on the block, it was tastefully so and served as an attractive backdrop to the quiet neighborhood.

When Josette first arrived, her parents received her as if she were a sight for their sore eyes. They were overjoyed to see that, physically at least, she was fit, and thought that a good dose of their loving would bring her back to herself. Lourdes cooked many of her special recipes, spicy tamales with white rice, fried *plaintanos* and a zesty *arroz con pollo* created with the perfect blend of chicken, sausage, bell peppers, garlic and tomatoes, which were among Josette's favorites. Lourdes spent an entire day preparing *pernier,* a slow-cooked piece of pork stuffed with rice, peppers and other seasonings. She hoped that the foods would be a comfort to Josette during the grieving process. Daily, Lourdes led Josette in prayer, asking for peace for the lost child and serenity for Josette and Seth. On her second night there, Benjamin brought home a twenty-pound catfish, which Lourdes pan-seared to perfection.

The thing that struck Josette the most was how much her parents had aged since she'd last seen them. They hadn't been able to make it to Marcus's graduation because her father had thrown his back out again and had been on complete bedrest for the entire month of June. They had flown out to New York the prior year for Simone's graduation, and the time between then and now seemed to have descended heavily upon them. While Lourdes's hair was no more gray than it had been for the past five years, and her skin was still smooth and virtually wrinkle free, her carriage seemed to have slowed down tremendously. Now she moved the way Josette remembered her grandmother moving. Her father, due to the chronic back problems he'd suffered for most of his adult life, now was slightly bent over when he stood and had difficulty rising from a chair or sitting down again. Some of the things that had not changed, however, were their good humor and sharp minds.

Josette tried to be jovial, more in an effort to appease her parents than because it was truly how she felt. She ate even when she didn't have an appetite, laughed when she didn't find anything funny, and talked when she'd rather silently sulk. She did not delve into the subject of her problems with Seth, but it was only a matter of time before her parents, especially her mother, picked up on the fact that something was amiss. That time came over breakfast on the fourth day of her visit.

"Is Daddy gone already?" Josette asked.

It was just after seven o'clock in the morning and despite the fact that she'd had a pretty restless night, she had been drawn from her old bedroom by the smell of her mother's cooking. She thought that she'd already gained five pounds since she'd arrived, but she didn't really care at this point. She entered the kitchen to find her mother seated at the cluttered table with Mrs. Robinson, a neighbor from two houses down the street.

"Yes, *niña*. He and your uncle George got an early start this morning. They'll be back by supper-time."

Lourdes removed an already-prepared plate from the microwave and set it at the table.

"Good morning, Mrs. Robinson," Josette said,

kissing the brown, creased forehead of the woman before taking a seat at the table.

"Josette, sweetie, you're looking good. Your mama told me that you were here. How've you been? Girl, that Big Apple must be treating you well, because you look fabulous!"

Mrs. Robinson had always been a talker. Josette remembered when she was a little girl and Mrs. Robinson would come to visit on Saturday evenings. She would talk and talk, gossiping about folks in the neighborhood, her husband's family, or whomever else she could think of. She would talk for hours and, save for an occasional grunt from Lourdes, hers would be the only voice heard for long stretches at a time. Josette would sit outside of the kitchen, her back flat against the wall as she tried to be invisible, listening and giggling at Mrs. Robinson's dialect and her antics.

That was another remarkable thing about the Medwala household. There were so many different nationalities that appeared at any given time on their doorstep. Besides their family's own mixed heritage, they had friends of various cultures and backgrounds. Mrs. Robinson, who was African-American, was married to a white Guyanese man. Josette had grown to love the potluck soup that was her home and credited that type of upbringing for the fact that today, she found it so easy to relate to each and every client who landed in her office, no matter what their background.

"Well, thank you, Mrs. Robinson. I don't know…. Maybe it's something in that New York water." Josette smiled.

"How's that husband of yours…Seth, isn't it? I'm surprised he's not out here visiting with you."

"He's doing fine—busy at work is all. Maybe next time," Josette said, visibly bristling at the mention of Seth.

"Josette, when are you going to cut the crap and tell us what's going on?" Lourdes said, taking a short sip from her second cup of coffee for the morning.

"Mami!" Josette exclaimed, glancing from her mother to Mrs. Robinson.

Her face flushed with unnecessary embarrassment. Little did she know that Lourdes and Mrs. Robinson had already discussed her at length.

"There's no need for you to act shy in front of Ernestine. She changed your diapers, you know. Now, what the hell is going on?"

"Ma, Seth and I are just having some difficulties, that's all. Nothing for anyone to worry about."

"Humph! Any time a woman packs up and comes clear across the country, I'd say that's something to worry about," Mrs. Robinson said.

Josette looked from one woman to the other, wishing that they could just drop the conversation, but she knew that was about as likely as it was that she would be dubbed Queen of England. She returned her fork to the plate, leaned back in her chair and folded her hands in her lap.

"Ladies, listen. I came out here because I needed a break. After the baby…I just needed to get away for a while. Seth and I, we just don't see eye to eye on things right now."

"What things?" Lourdes asked, her eyes narrowing as she looked at her daughter.

"Well, the baby was one, for instance. Seth did not want the baby. He was not at all happy about it and that was hard for me to deal with," Josette admitted.

"I don't blame that man. You two have grown children.… Simone is in her second year of college and Marcus is off now, too. Why would he want to start all over again…changing diapers and fixing Big Wheels," Lourdes stated emphatically.

"I know that's right. When Junior left for the army, my Samuel practically nailed the door shut behind him. Now, we loved having him.… Junior was a good kid and grew up to be a fine young man, but there's nothing like being carefree and having your home back to yourself. Now, when Junior comes by, bringing the grandbabies, we love to have them and we love to see them go home," Mrs. Robinson said, cackling aloud.

"But, Mrs. Robinson, Ma, you don't understand. We didn't plan to have the baby, true, but once he was there, growing inside of me… I don't know, I just expected Seth to be happier about it. It was *our* baby."

"I understand what you're saying, *niña,* but did

you at least try to understand it from Seth's point of view?" Lourdes asked softly.

Josette sat quietly, thinking about what her mother said. She had considered all the implications of having the baby, and she'd known that it would dramatically change the rest of their lives. She had been able to squash her fears and adjust to the idea almost instantly. However, maybe she had been unfair to Seth, expecting him to adjust as quickly as she had.

"Josette, you need to talk to your husband and try to understand him. That man loves you and has always taken good care of you. From the moment you and he got married, your dad and I stopped worrying. We just knew that you would have a good life and that Seth would do everything in his power to keep you happy."

"Mami, I would love to talk to Seth. Unfortunately, Seth has found someone else to talk to," Josette blurted, the true source of her anguish finally coming to the surface.

"What do you mean, someone else? What are you talking about, Josette?"

Josette explained everything from the e-mails to the lack of intimacy they had been experiencing previously. She told them about the sex therapist she had been seeing, expressing how she had believed things to be getting better between them until the baby had come along. By the time she was finished, she was in tears again. She had promised herself she wouldn't cry again but the mere mention of Seth's betrayal reduced her to a blub-bering idiot.

The elder women let her have her moment, handing her Kleenex and ordering her to blow her nose. Finally, when she seemed to have gained control over her emotions, Lourdes lit in to her.

"Josette, are you stupid?" she asked.

Josette looked sharply at her mother, bewildered by her tone. She glanced over at Mrs. Robinson, who was now cracking up with laughter.

"Boy, you young women nowadays are some-thing else," Mrs. Robinson said.

"Ernestine, you've got that one right. They don't know nothing, but swear they know everything," Lourdes agreed. To Josette she added, "Josette, I really thought I taught you better than that. First of all, how in the hell did you let things go in your bedroom? You might as well have dressed your man up and set him out with the trash. Of course some needy woman would roll up in her pickup truck and toss him into the back."

"Are you blaming me?" Josette asked, insulted and shocked at the same moment.

"We're not blaming you, sweetheart, but you should have known better. You've got yourself a good man and if you love him the way you claim to, you would be making sure that his needs are being met—by you. Baby, when a man is being taken care of, I mean really taken care of, then his woman's world is golden."

"How so?" Josette asked.

She tried to remain objective even though she doubted seriously that these two old women had any clue as to what they were talking about.

"Because a satisfied man will do everything in his power to make sure his woman is satisfied. In other words, meeting his needs guarantees that yours will be met, as well. It's very simple," Lourdes said.

Josette looked from her mother's face to the serious expression of Mrs. Robinson, who was nodding her head up and down.

"Mami, I don't mean to be disrespectful, but you can't be serious?" Josette asked.

"There you go again, Josette, thinking you know everything while you really don't know anything. I know you think I sound like something out of the dark ages. I know you also think that women have more options than ever before and that to be subservient to your husband is out of the question for a modern woman."

"Well, if that's how you want to put it…" Josette agreed.

"Let me tell you something, Miss Lady. A woman's role *is* to be subservient to her man. Read your Bible and you'll see it's the truth. Nobody is saying that you are to be ruled or governed by your man and nobody is trying to make a woman out to be less than she is. A woman is the mightiest creature on this good earth. God knew what he was doing and you have no right to question his judgment."

"Oh, don't be melodramatic! I'm not questioning God's judgment, Mami," Josette defended.

She stood up from the table, annoyed by the conversation and wanting desperately just to go back upstairs. Breakfast forgotten, she wanted to be alone.

"Sit down and listen to me," her mother commanded.

Despite the fact that she was forty-six years old, Josette had the good sense to obey. She was raised to believe that disrespecting one's mother would guarantee a one-way trip to hell.

"Yes, Mami," she answered.

"Josette, Seth was wrong to seek comfort from someone else besides you. You are his wife, and he should come to you first and foremost for anything and everything that he needs. But sweetheart, you have to understand how a man thinks. He is not rational or logical when it comes to his heart. He does not have a woman's ability to reason. Like a child, when he is hurt he seeks comfort. When he is angry, he seeks vengeance. When he is lost, he'll let himself be taken in by anyone who is willing to open the door for him. All I'm saying to you is that you should never have allowed him to be hurt, angry or lost. It is you, his wife, who keeps him from that. That is why a man seeks a woman in the first place.

He knows that he cannot maintain that balance on his own."

Lourdes took her daughter's hand in hers, seeing that she needed to be touched, yet sensing that she needed to be scolded even more. She understood her daughter's pain more than she knew, more than she would ever tell her. She'd been through her own dark hours with her husband, and she had stood her ground, consequently saving her marriage. In a world that was full of chaos and strife, where good sometimes took a swift butt-kicking from evil, Lourdes knew what it took to stay strong and to persevere. She hated that her daughter had had to face hard times, but she also knew that her child had found a man and a marriage that were worth fighting for.

"Sweetheart, listen to me good now. A wife is more than a title. A wife is a husband's center, his life force. You are Seth's rock...and you are his world. Everything that he has done and the man that he has become is in great part because of you, and that is true for you, as well. Seth was not seeking a warm body or sex. He was trying to find balance.... Nothing more."

Josette considered her mother's words without speaking. In her brain, everything her mother had just said made perfect sense, but her heart was having a hard time connecting the dots.

"You and Seth have built a fantastic life together. He is successful because he had you in his corner.

Your grown children are beautiful because they had a mother to nurture them. What is so wrong with Seth wanting you all to himself now? What is so bad about his appreciating all that you have done for him and his family and now wanting to spend your later years wrapped up in one another, enjoying the fruits of your labor?"

"Nothing, I suppose. But why couldn't he just say that to me? Why'd he have to talk to someone else about it?"

"Would you have listened to him, Josette? Be honest," Mrs. Robinson chimed in. "One of our biggest problems as women is that sometimes, when we know we're right, we stick cotton in our ears and block out everything and everybody."

"I hear you, Mami...Mrs. Robinson. Thank you, ladies, for what you've said. I...I'm going to go lie back down for a little while. My stomach's a little upset," Josette said, excusing herself from the kitchen.

That afternoon, her mother brought up a piping-hot bowl of her homemade chicken-noodle soup. Josette polished off two helpings, grateful for having a mother who was equally as wise as she was a master in the kitchen. Unexpectedly, Josette had learned that the wisdom of sister girls cannot be denied and when that wisdom comes from mothers and grandmothers, it is more valuable than the purest black diamond.

Josette spent the remainder of her visit helping

her mother out with various craft projects she had going on simultaneously around the house, including reupholstering the armchairs in the den and planting perennials in the newly structured front garden. She also went fishing with her father and, true to form, he sat by her side in virtual silence for hours, few but priceless jewels falling from his lips. His strength became her strength as she shared that time with him, making her even more grateful that she had come home when she had. She also visited her mother's eldest sister, Aunt Lulu, who was seventy-four and happily married to a former heavyweight boxer who was almost half her age. Aunt Lulu was as feisty and rambunctious as ever, delighting Josette with her stories.

By the time her visit with her parents drew to a close, Josette was feeling much better and was looking forward to seeing Seth again. She was uncertain if she had gotten over the hurt he'd caused her or if she truly would be able to in the near future, but she was very sure that she wanted and needed to be with her husband. She recognized that she had been unfair to Seth by not validating his concerns and misgivings about the baby in the first place. She had been so wrapped up in her own feelings that she had not even asked him how he felt about it. She did not know if she was as courageous or if she would ever be as wise as her mother and the women before her. She did know that her marriage was worth more than a try. It was worth

everything to her. She looked forward to seeing
Seth face-to-face, and hoped that in time they
would find a way to reconcile and move on with
their life together.

Chapter 24

Two weeks turned out to be a longer separation than it had seemed to Josette. It was long enough to create an even bigger wedge between her and Seth, and Josette returned to find the tables had turned. Seth had had time to stew in his own juices, and he was feeling angry and betrayed by her departure. He met her at the airport and was noticeably reserved. She chatted nervously, filling him in on her parents, the rest of her family and the zany neighbors whom she'd gotten a chance to see during her visit. She described the festival she'd gone to where she'd watched talented dancers perform the *viejitos* and the *huapango,* the latter of which Seth had learned to do very well when they'd vacationed in Mexico years ago. He barely grunted as she spoke, and her attempts to engage him in conversation failed miserably.

By the time they arrived at their home, Josette was determined to be direct and sit down with Seth to put their issues on the table. To her surprise, however, Simone was waiting at the front door.

"Mommy, you're home!" she exclaimed, throwing her arms around Josette's body. "You look great, Mom," she said.

"Thank you, baby. It's good to see you. I wasn't expecting you home, though. Is something wrong?"

"Why does something have to be wrong for me to come home?" Simone said, grabbing the small bag that Josette carried in her hand and leading her mother inside.

"Nothing has to be wrong, but didn't you tell us over the holidays that we probably wouldn't see you until spring break—what with the overload of classes you're taking this semester and your job and all your activities?"

"I know, I know, but I had to come and check on you. I called Dad yesterday, and he told me that you'd be coming in this afternoon. I got someone to cover for me at work and hopped in the car."

"Ooh, look at you being so sweet! But, honey, it's my job to worry about you—not the other way around. Are you hungry?" Josette asked, switching into mother mode as soon as her footsteps crossed the threshold.

She went to the master bedroom to change out of her traveling clothes, and was struck immediately by how unchanged the room was. The calico spread and half a dozen decorative pillows still covered their king-size bed exactly as she had left it. In all the years she and Seth had been together, he had never once taken the time to arrange the pillows in this neat a fashion. She new instantly that he had not lain on that bed at any moment during her absence from home. This truth struck her oddly, making her feel guilty, but at the same time unwelcomed suspicion crept into her brain. She shook the latter emotion off, eager to keep all negative feelings at bay as she tried to reconnect with her husband.

Josette changed into a pair of baby-pink velour sweatpants and a plain white Gap T-shirt. She pulled her hair back with her hands and tied a black scrunchie around it. In the master bathroom, she washed her face in lukewarm water, applied a thin layer of moisturizer and headed back downstairs. Before descending the stairs, she glanced at the closed door of the guest bedroom. Feeling compelled, she approached the door, listened against it for a moment, and, hearing nothing, she opened it slightly. With one look at the queen-size four-poster bed, she knew where Seth had spent his time while she had been away. She closed the door again and continued downstairs.

Seth and Simone's voices carried from the den, where they had installed themselves in front of the plasma television that hung from the room's south wall. Josette stood in the hallway outside of the den, listening to the chatter between father and daughter. Seth's booming laughter rang out, bouncing off the walls as he responded to something Simone had said. Simone had always been able to make Seth laugh, even over the most silly, grossly unfunny things. There was a bond between those two that was equally as fascinating as it was enviable. Calling her *daddy's little girl* was an understatement. She was more like his alter ego. As a baby, Simone hadn't fussed over a soiled diaper, had waited patiently until her bottles were prepared and had giggled and cooed as she enjoyed being bathed at any time of the day or night. The thing that had struck Josette most was the way that Simone's little eyes would light up whenever Seth came home from work. As soon as she'd heard his voice, calling out to her or to her mother, she'd grown excited, flailing her little arms all around and making noises that sounded like cheers of "Hurrah!" As she'd grown into a little girl, she'd become the most even-tempered child Josette had ever seen. She'd rarely cried and had almost never complained. Still, her eyes had shone like black coals when her daddy was around. The more her vocabulary had grown, the more anecdotes and jokes she'd found to entertain with, many of them reserved for Seth. The two of them had become inseparable and Josette had looked on with pride as she'd watched Seth become his little girl's hero and she, his biggest source of pride.

Hearing them now made Josette remember how good their life really was. There were so many children and parents who were out of reach of one another, with no clue as to how to come together again. They were a tight-knit, loving family. Those warm thoughts carried her on to the kitchen, where she retrieved a bag of extra-large shrimp from the freezer. Grateful that she had previously had the presence of mind to clean, devein and season the shrimp before freezing them, she spent the next thirty minutes making shrimp enchiladas. When it was ready, she carried the scrumptious dish into the den, setting it down on the desk. Simone dug right in, never having been one to let a good meal sit too long.

Over dinner, Simone informed them that Connor had invited her down to Virginia to visit his grandmother during spring break.

"Would it be okay if I went?" she asked.

Seth loved the fact that unlike most young people nowadays, both of his children still asked their permission or opinions before doing things, and didn't just inform them of what their plans were. He was about to nod his head in approval, but Josette's stern look caused him to pause.

"Simone, I really don't think it's a good idea for

you to be getting serious right now. With school and everything...I don't want you to lose focus," Josette said.

"Ma, what are you talking about?" Simone asked, a forkful of cheesy enchilada poised before her lips.

"Well, I mean...Connor is a nice young man, and I couldn't be more pleased to know you're spending time with someone like him. But you've been talking quite a bit about him and you two seem to spend a lot of time together. Your father and I were talking, and we just hope that you're not getting too wrapped up in him."

Simone looked at her father, whose face held the expression of someone who didn't really want to weigh in on this particular conversation.

"Mom, you are absolutely right. Connor and I have been spending a lot of time together, and I really like him. However, I can assure you that you have nothing to worry about. Connor is just as serious about his studies as I am, if not more. He's carrying a double major, works in the school's computer-technology lab and most of the time when we're together, we're studying or typing papers. He's good company, and he also helps me stay focused."

Simone's earnest expression was not lost on Josette nor Seth. Josette remained silent for a moment, wanting to choose her next words carefully. Her daughter, beautiful, intelligent and sensitive, was now a woman. Of that she was certain. What could she say, woman to woman, that would be wise and thought-provoking, but would not come off sounding opinionated and scolding? Before Josette could speak, however, Seth finally found his tongue and stepped in.

"That's good to know, sweetheart, but… I guess what your mother is trying to say is that we've just never seen you so involved with one person. Is there something we should be looking forward to?"

"Something like what? A wedding?" Simone asked incredulously.

"Well—" Josette began.

"Pump your brakes, Ma. That is so not on our minds right now. I mean, guys, I'm a sophomore. I've got two more years of undergrad, then grad school and who knows what after that. I'm not about to tie the knot with anyone, so you don't have to worry about that."

Josette raised her hands in surrender, realizing that her daughter's mind was on the right track, and worrying about her was unnecessary. As evening approached, Josette packed a plastic bowl of leftovers for Simone and sent her on the road back to school. As she watched her daughter back out of the driveway, she felt an awesome pride at having raised such a beautiful child. She also felt somewhat nostalgic for the time in her own life where things were so uncomplicated and clear.

Josette returned to dance class that week, feeling

as if she desperately needed to work out some of
the tension she had been holding in her mind and
body. Natalie accompanied her to Mama Sa's class.
Mama Sa greeted Josette back like an old auntie.

"Where ya been, child?"

"I was ill, but I'm doing much better now,"
Josette responded.

"All right then. Let's see if we can't work some
of that sickness out of your body tonight. Is that
all right?"

Mama Sa draped an arm around Josette, leading
the smiling woman to the front line of the class.
Mama Sa nodded to the drummers, who began
tapping out a slow, rhythmic beat for the class to
warm up to. Mama Sa led them in the ritual warm-
up and Josette immediately felt as though she were
back home and had never left. Her mind shut down
and her heart opened up as her body responded in-
stinctively. Seventy-five minutes later, Josette felt
as light as a feather, heart and soul. The class
clapped for the drummers, giving the usual thank-
yous orally before breaking for the drummers to
beat out a one-minute closing.

"Josette, you looked fantastic up there, practically leading the class," Clint said.

"Thank you, Clint," Josette said, smiling and
looking up at him.

Natalie stood between the two, feeling like a
third wheel. She raised a brow at Josette, waiting
for her to get the hint.

"Oh, forgive me…. Natalie, this Clinton Parks, Mr. Parks—"

"Clint," he corrected.

"Clint, this is my good friend and colleague, Natalie Alexander."

"Nice to meet you," Natalie said as she took Clint's extended hand, shaking it warmly.

"So, Miss Josette, I was beginning to think you'd gone off somewhere and started your own dance studio," Clint joked.

"Nah, I'm not that good. I don't think anyone would pay me to teach them my little two-step."

"I would," he said.

The ensuing silence was charged with intensity as the three of them stood looking at one another.

"Well, ladies, are you headed home for the evening or could I interest you in having a cup of coffee with me?" Clint asked.

Josette glanced at Natalie, whose mouth smiled but her eyes registered unmistakable disapproval.

"I don't see why we couldn't have one quick cup," Josette stated, ignoring Natalie's silent message.

"Great. Let's go then."

Clint led the way out of the studio and into the corridor. There was a large crowd waiting for the building's one small elevator, so he suggested that they take the stairs. As they headed into the narrow stairwell, Clint in front and the two women following behind, Natalie tugged at Josette's sleeve.

"What's up?" she hissed through clenched teeth.

"It's just coffee, Natalie," Josette replied in a whisper.

Natalie's expression remained skeptical and tight, but she refrained from saying anything further.

The trio walked a block over to Twenty-third Street, where they found a Starbucks that was only minimally crowded. At the counter they ordered their drinks and then found a small table with high stools near the front door.

"Tell me, Mr. Parks—" Natalie began once they were settled.

"Clint," he corrected again.

"Clint. Tell me, Clint, have you been studying African dance long?"

"No, not really. I'd been talking about needing some exercise and a friend of mine who is from Kenya recommended that I take a dance class. She actually teaches one herself, but she's all the way out on Long Island. She pointed me in the direction of Dyobi Studios, so one night I decided to check it out."

"I see. Well, you seem to be getting the hang of it," Natalie said.

"Oh yeah, I love it. I mean, normally, when I think of working out I think of all of those Nike outfit-clad clones, with the iPods tucked in their pockets, running on a treadmill for thirty minutes a day. Definitely not my idea of a good time.

African dance is fun and different. I'm telling you, in these past few weeks I have worked parts that I'd forgotten were there."

"Yeah, you're having fun, but are you getting in shape?" Josette smiled.

Natalie flashed a surprised look, marveling at the girlish quality in her friend's voice.

"I feel like it. Now, I haven't noticed any extra room in my clothing, but I guess that's going to take a little more time." Clint laughed, Josette's ringing giggle chiming in with him.

Natalie sipped her green-tea Frappuccino silently as she watched this exchange. Just when she thought that she would burst from holding her tongue for so long, Clint's cell phone rang.

"Oh, I've been waiting on this call. Excuse me for a moment, ladies," he said as he rose from his stool and moved closer to the door.

"Uh, Josette, what's going on?" Natalie said softly.

"What are you talking about, Natalie?" Josette replied, looking her square in the eye.

"Josette, you cannot be serious. If this guy flirted any harder with you, he'd get slapped with an indecency charge and you…you're sitting here eating it up like whipped-cream-covered cherry pie!"

"Natalie!"

Josette glanced at Clint, who was still talking into his cell phone.

"Don't *Natalie* me. You know that man's got a thing for you. He's obvious as hell and doesn't seem to care who knows it. I thought you said you only saw him the one time?"

"That's the truth…. Just the one night in class when you were sick. Despite what your overactive imagination has cooked up, there is nothing going on between Clint and me. He struck up a conversation and we hit it off, true, but that's all there is to it. I'm a married woman, you know."

"Oh, I know it. I'm just not too sure that you know it these days."

Before Josette could voice her displeasure at Natalie's last biting comment, Clint returned to the table.

"So, Clint, pretty late in the day to be conducting business, isn't it?" Natalie queried.

"No, not really. That was my brother calling from Paris. It's three o'clock in the morning there. I've been trying to catch up with him all week because I was supposed to be taking a trip out to see him and his new wife and baby next month. I couldn't complete my travel plans until I checked some things with him. He's been up in the mountains hiking for the past few days, so I've been waiting on his call."

"Paris? Wow, what took him all the way over there to live?" Josette asked.

Clint talked excitedly for a while about his brother, Preston, who was a professor of historical and cultural studies at the American University of Paris. Preston and his daughter from a prior marriage had gone on vacation together to France four years ago, where he'd met a French journalist. They'd dated for all of two weeks before eloping. Preston had never returned to the United States save for brief visits.

Chapter 25

Josette used her spoon to scoop a chunk of whipped cream from the top of her steaming-hot cup of cocoa. Seated across from Clint, she hated the fact that she was feeling very reluctant to go home. As the days passed since she'd returned from California, she had been racking her brain trying to figure out a way to smooth the rocky road between her and Seth. While the tension seemed to have dissipated, it was still as if an invisible barrier had been erected between them, and she was at a loss as to how to climb over it, under it or to tear it down altogether. They had been talking, tentatively, to one another about everything under the sun except their relationship. He'd been working late almost every night and while she knew that he had a lot on his plate, she also believed that he was choosing to keep his distance. Josette knew that something had to give soon because the space was hurting both of them tremendously.

Tonight, however, she just didn't want to go home to an empty house. Once again, she was reminded of how much she had come to depend on her family. The laughter and the companionship she found with her husband and children was irreplaceable, and it was something that she needed as much as she needed food to eat and air to breath. She didn't want to keep imposing on Natalie, taking her away from her own family. Nardo had not returned from his trip yet and, while Josette had considered hooking up with other girlfriends, she didn't really feel like being around people who knew her history. She didn't really want to talk about her problems, and she knew they would all ask.

With a troubled mind that needed escape, even if it were only momentary, she'd once again accepted Clint's invitation for coffee. Chatting with him now, she appreciated the distraction.

"So, Clint, you've never mentioned kids. Do you have any?" she asked.

"Nope. Was never in the cards, I guess," he answered.

"That's too bad. It's definitely an experience. I have two," Josette said.

"Yes, Simone and Marcus, right?"

"I suppose I talk about them too much, huh?" Josette blushed.

"No, not at all. It's nice to hear a proud mama brag every now and then. The media bombards us with images of kids gone bad all the time. Your success stories with your kids are a welcome sound-bite."

"Thank you."

"It's funny. You never think that you won't have an opportunity to do something until one day you look up and realize that time has passed you by."

"Nonsense. You know a man can have a baby well up into his sixties. Look at Michael Douglas and Tony Randall."

"No, thank you. I'm not about to roll up to my kid's soccer game in a wheelchair with an oxygen tank hooked up to me." Clint laughed.

Josette joined him, acknowledging that she did think that some of these celebrities should have quit while they were ahead.

"Besides, there's really only been one woman in my life whom I'd considered having kids with. My wife, Cheryl."

"You're married?" Josette asked.

She didn't know why she was surprised by the admission. After all, she was married, too, yet here she was sitting in a coffee shop with a man whom her husband knew nothing about. It was just that after what Natalie had said, Josette had given it a little thought and realized that maybe she was right. On the one hand, Clint seemed like just a nice guy being friendly, but on the other, there were subtle hints that maybe he was looking for more than friendship. Finding out that he was married and flirting just took his character down a few notches in her book.

"Was married," he clarified. "I lost Cheryl five years ago."

"Oh, I'm so sorry, Clint," Josette said, chiding herself for thinking the worst of him.

"Thank you. It was hard, but it was a blessing, too. She'd been suffering for quite a while and seeing her like that was the toughest thing I ever had to do. We had thought that we had all the time in the world to have kids...until she was struck with multiple sclerosis. The degeneration happened so fast that we didn't know what hit us. She was only forty when she finally lost the battle."

"That's terrible for you. And you've been single ever since?"

"Yep. I mean, I date a little, but I was never much into that scene. Cheryl and I had been married for ten years and I guess she's just a hard act to follow."

"Well, you know that no one will ever be able to replace her. All you can hope is that you find someone who complements who you are and shares your dreams for the future."

"That's easier said than done. Times seem so

different now. Everybody's out for themselves now, wanting to know what you can give them, what they can get from you. It's so rare to see people just falling in love without a plan or calculated effort. You've got all these Internet dating services and whatnot. And then, when people do match up, it doesn't last. I mean, what is the secret to staying in love today once you find it?"

She considered Clint's question before answering, not because she was reluctant to answer it but more because she did not know how to answer it.

"I don't think it's really a matter of staying in love as opposed to continuously falling in love. I mean, people change. That's a fact and no matter what you think you know about a person, tomorrow that person could say or do something that you would not have expected. You spend years together and while you love the person you married, I think that you have to expect that the person is constantly evolving."

"That said, are you saying that a person's character changes?"

Clint watched Josette take a careful sip from her now-naked cocoa, enjoying the way she pursed her lips together to do so. This woman was beautiful. Admittedly, there were things about her that reminded him of Cheryl, the wife he'd buried but had yet to stop missing tremendously. However, it was more than a physical resemblance that had attracted him to her. Josette was a wholesome, beautiful woman. She was understated, not overly made-up or adorned like many women in their age group tended to do in order to give the appearance of being younger. Without any additives, Josette was a gorgeous woman who looked as if she was comfortable in her skin, just as it was. That aspect of her had caused him to pay more attention to her than he had to the dance instructor that first night in dance class.

"No, I don't think that's the case. Your character—the beliefs you hold and the way you carry yourself—doesn't change. At least not dramatically. But I think that as a person grows and moves into different phases in his or her life, that person is bound to change. For example, at twenty a woman is just coming into her own, you know? She's learning to love herself, accept who she is and start to chart her own destiny. She will not be the same woman twenty years later because of the experiences she goes through. She may have different hopes and dreams, different realities."

"I'm not sure if men are that complicated," Clint mused.

"They definitely are. A twenty-year-old male is a boy. I look at my son—he's almost nineteen years old—and even though he's a mature and responsible individual, he's nowhere near being a man. I can look at him with iron-clad confidence, however, knowing that based on the foundation that has been laid and the qualities that he shows now, he will be a fine man one day. Not today, but in a few years. Now think about that—a woman who falls in love with Marcus today will not get to know the man he will become for quite some time, and by the time she does, she may not like him."

"That's a very interesting philosophy, Miss Josette. So have you mastered this trick of constantly renewing love?"

"Sometimes…I think so. It's an ongoing process and sometimes, you and your mate could be at a place where everything is good. You're vibing with each other and he is who you need him to be and vice versa. But there are other times when you wonder…" Josette's voice trailed off.

She looked away from Clint, feeling as if she'd said too much already.

"Which phase are you in right now?" Clint persisted.

He wanted to know if he stood a chance or if Josette's heart was too full for him.

"What are you asking me, Clint?"

Typical Josette, he thought. She was a person who could be counted on to cut right to the quick of things. That was another trait of hers that he found alluring. He smiled, realizing that now was the time for him to put up or shut up.

"I'm asking you if you're happy in your marriage. If you tell me yes, I'd tell you that I'm happy for you and wish you twenty more years of wedded bliss. However, if you say that you're not…well then I'd probably ask what you intend to do about that. I'd also want to know if you'd like to go out to dinner with me some time."

Josette's face flushed noticeably as she confirmed her suspicions that Clint was interested in her. Despite what Natalie had said, Josette had been trying to convince herself that she was too old to have a man hitting on her, yet here it was. There was no denying or downplaying Clint's attraction to her. After dance class tonight, he'd invited both her and Natalie out for coffee again, but when Natalie had begged off and Josette had not, there'd been was a noticeable gleam in his eyes.

"Clint, I don't know what to say," Josette began.

"I know what I'd like you to say, but only you know what is right for you," he responded.

"My husband, Seth, and I are going through a rough patch right now. It's been a trying few months to say the least, but even if we were calling it quits, and believe me, I have not thought that far ahead yet, the last thing I would be looking for would be another relationship."

Josette studied Clint's face, looking for a reaction and feeling embarrassed when she saw the slightly crestfallen countenance. He was a man whose handsome face was completely open. Any woman who had eyes could read his heart if she really looked at him. It was obvious that she had not given him the answer he was looking for.

"I'm sorry, Clint," she said.

"Don't be. It's nice to see a committed woman such as yourself."

He took a sip from his cup, swallowing it pensively. He looked into Josette's eyes with the sincerity of a man who loved hard when he loved.

"You are a silver moon casting light on a heart's valleys—a welcome intrusion for however long you deign to shine," he said, his eyes bright and penetrating.

The small coffee shop was quiet that night, the few patrons silently enjoying their snacks and beverages and the television's volume turned down to a low decibel. These were the thoughts that struck Josette at that moment, replaced by the opposing thought that maybe everything seemed the have faded into the background as the poetry of his words demanded front and center on the stage of her mind. In that moment, for that fraction of time, all she felt was a supreme and encompassing femininity. She felt like a woman—desirable and beautiful.

Clint reached over, placing his hand on hers. She looked down at his warm, brown hand that covered her own.

"Clint—"

"I'm sorry, Josette. I don't mean to be disrespectful in any way. I know that you're a married woman, and I would never do anything to sully the sacredness of that. I just had to tell you what was in my heart."

"I appreciate that, Clint," she said, not removing her hand immediately.

She sighed.

"Can't blame a man for wishing, can you?"

"In another lifetime," she began, trailing off because she did not need to finish the statement.

Clint caught the meaning in her eyes and, as they were the window to her soul, he knew what rested in her heart. He hoped that her man knew how fortunate he was. He squeezed her hand once quickly and then withdrew it.

"I'm content with being a friend…at least I hope you consider me that much. An occasional cup of coffee after Mama Sa works the calories off of us?"

"I'd love to count you as a friend, Clint," Josette said, smiling and leaning back in her chair. She swallowed the remaining drips of cocoa, her thoughts floating up the road to her home and her husband, and just as she returned the mug to the table, her cell phone rang.

Chapter 26

Josette could barely form the words to explain to Clint what was happening. She made a mad dash from the coffee shop and he followed. At the corner of Eighth Avenue, he hailed a yellow cab and opened the door for her. She slid in and, despite her protests, he jumped in beside her.

She implored the driver to hurry as she filled Clint in on what was going on. It seemed the phone call had been from Seth. He'd been whispering, and she could barely make out his words. He was in his office building, and had just been getting ready to leave for the night when a man had appeared with a gun in the office, shouting. Presently, he was trapped in a corner of the firm's library with a couple of colleagues and he was concerned for their safety. He'd told her that he'd just wanted to hear her voice one more time. Before she could comprehend what he'd been saying to her, the phone had gone dead.

While the cab sped downtown, Clint advised her to call the police. She dialed 911 and, after holding for several minutes, she was transferred to a detective. Apparently, they were already aware of the situation and, according to the officer, they had police on the scene and were expecting to bring an end to the crisis shortly. They implored her to go home and await further news, but there was no way she was going to do that.

About a block from the office building, they hit stalled traffic. The block had been corded off and no one was being allowed to drive any closer. Josette and Clint jumped out of the taxi and made their way through the crowded streets on foot. They got within one hundred feet of the front door of the office building before being stopped by police.

"You don't understand. My husband is in there. He's in some sort of trouble," she said, her voice trembling with emotion.

"What is your name, ma'am?" a female police officer asked.

"Josette Crawford. My husband is Seth Crawford. He's a senior partner at Waters, McLean, Berber and Crawford. He called me a few minutes ago and said that there's someone with a gun in his office. What's going on?"

Josette looked nervously around the sea of police officers clad in uniform and others in suits and other plainclothes. The flashing, spinning lights shining from the tops of the dozen or more patrol cars added intensity to the already electric scene.

"Mrs. Crawford, I'm Officer Patterson. We were called to the scene about thirty minutes ago. From what we've been able to figure out, we have one hostile individual inside, on the thirty-seventh floor of the building. He entered the offices of Waters, McLean, Berber and Crawford at approximately eight-fifteen tonight and demanded to see a woman. We are unclear as to his relationship to that woman."

"So you think that this is a domestic issue?" Josette asked.

"Well, we can't speculate on that right now," the officer said. "All we know thus far is that an argument ensued and at that point the individual brandished a weapon. We believe that one shot was fired almost twenty minutes ago and that's all we know."

"Oh, God!" Josette exclaimed, covering her mouth with trembling hands.

"Officer, are you in contact with anyone inside? I mean, her husband called her so obviously they have access to phones in there," Clint stated, draping his arm protectively around Josette.

"Sir, I really wish I could tell you more. Right now, that is all we know. I promise you that we're doing everything we can to bring this situation to a peaceful close."

The officer ushered Josette and Clint to a cluster of police cars to the right of the barricades in front of the building, asking them to wait until she came back for them. Josette leaned heavily against one of the cars, her face ashen as fear drained all of the color from her.

"Do you want me to call anyone?" Clint asked. "Natalie, maybe?"

He felt inadequate as he stood beside her, not knowing her well enough to know if she would be able to hold up under this enormous pressure. He suspected that the woman he was just beginning to get to know could handle any adversity, but he couldn't be sure. He wished that he could be of some comfort, offer some reassurance, but he had none to give.

The irony of the situation was that just a short while ago he had been making a move on the woman and now here he was holding her hand while her husband faced a life-or-death crisis. He knew that he should feel embarrassed, but somehow, he didn't. He was a man who believed that everything happened for a reason and while it presently seemed that he and Josette were not destined to be together as he had hoped, he was glad that he was in a position to support her in this way.

"No...no one. I can't call anyone until I know...until I know if he's—"

"Shh, Josette. Don't even think like that. I'm sure your husband is a smart man. He was ingenious enough to sneak a call to you, right?"

"Yeah. I can't believe he did that."

Josette wished that she could replay that phone call over and over again. She hated the thoughts that were encroaching on her sanity right now, but she could not help herself. That could very well be the last time she heard her husband's voice. Two decades of laughter, loving and living could all be over and all she had was the memory of his terrified last shout out to her. She wanted to kick herself silly for the past few weeks of torture that she'd contributed to in their marriage. If she hadn't known it before, she definitely knew it now—when faced with trials or tribulations, she was the one thing on Seth's mind. He'd wanted to hear her voice one more time. Those were his words and no more precious words had ever been uttered to her in her entire life.

At that moment, Josette closed her eyes, and she began to pray. It was a feverish prayer, emanating from the core of her being. She knew that her life would cease to hold meaning if Seth were taken away from her. She prayed that God would be merciful on him and on her, taking away all of the hard-heartedness of the past few weeks. She prayed that at that moment Seth knew how much she loved him, knew that she was down there waiting on him, and somehow, found the strength, courage and wisdom to make it through this ordeal and come back to her.

She opened her eyes, her faith renewed. She saw Clint standing in front of her, studying her face.

"He's going to be fine," she said softly.

Then, with more conviction, she added, "He's going to be just fine. You don't know Seth. He's probably up there sweet-talking that guy, conning him out of his gun and everything else. He's smooth…my husband. Everybody likes him. It's hard not to." She smiled. "No, he's going to be just fine."

"I'm sure you're right, Josette. Just keep on believing that."

The wait seemed interminable. A team of specially trained crisis-tactics officers arrived, swooping into the building like a mighty army of ninjas. When the news cameras arrived, Josette realized that it was time to make phone calls. She couldn't risk her family finding out about the situation from their televisions. The first call she made was to Simone because she was the closest and the one more likely to receive the local news.

"Simone, it's Mommy," she said.

"What's up, Ma? Are you all right? You sound funny," Simone answered.

"Listen, baby, I need to talk to you about something important. There's a situation here…. I don't want you to get alarmed. Everything's going to be all right," Josette said, feeling completely inadequate at this point.

"Ma, you're scaring me. What's going on?"

"There's a crisis in your father's office building and he's stuck up there, but the police are here and they're going to get him out real soon."

"What kind of a crisis? What do you mean he's stuck? What are you talking about, Ma?" Simone shouted.

Josette could hear the panic as it seeped into Simone's voice, and she wished that she hadn't had to make the call at all. However, she knew what she had to do and so she forged ahead.

"A man showed up at the office and appeared to be very angry about something. Your father just happened to still be there and now the guy won't let anyone leave."

"Why can't they leave? Mommy, is he armed?" Simone asked.

"Yes, he is, but, baby, listen. Your dad called me and he told me not to worry. They are talking to the guy and this thing is expected to be over in just a short while. I just don't want you to see anything on the news and be upset. Trust me, I'm down here, right outside of the building, and the news reporters have no idea what's going on. I'm talking directly to the police, and I know that things are not as bad as the news will make them out to be," Josette said.

She hated to have to lie to her daughter, but she

was not about to have her freaking out. It was her job to do the worrying for this family.

"Ma, I'm coming up there. I—"

"No!" Josette shouted. "You are absolutely not to do that. I mean it, Simone. The last thing I need is to be worried about you driving like a madwoman trying to get up here. There is nothing you can do here and like I said, by the time you get here, this thing will be over and Daddy and I will be safe at home. Do you hear me, young lady?" Josette said, using her mother voice.

"But, Ma…"

"Simone! Is Connor there with you?" she asked.

"Yes, he is."

"Let me speak with him," she commanded.

"Mrs. Crawford. Hey, what's going on?" Connor asked.

"Listen, Connor, there's a bit of a situation going on down here…. Simone will fill you in. But what I want you to do is promise me that under no circumstances will you let her come up here. I absolutely forbid it. So I need you to keep her calm and make her stay put."

"All right, Mrs. Crawford. If you're sure," he answered, detecting the seriousness of her request.

"I'm sure. Now I know my daughter, and I don't care what she says to you or how she threatens you, you keep her butt down there."

"Yes, ma'am."

Josette spoke briefly to Simone again and then

hung up, first promising to call her within the hour with an update. While that call had completely exhausted her, she knew that she had more calls to make. She called Marcus next, who was much calmer than she'd expected. Ironically, he said that he had been on the Internet and there was breaking news about the incident. He hadn't recognized the address right off as his father's office. He, too, made her promise that she'd call him back within the hour to tell him what was happening, which she did.

The next phone call was to Seth's father. Together, they decided not to tell his wife because, as she was suffering from kidney failure, she did not need the stress. She had already gone to bed for the evening so there was no chance that she'd see the news. Ernest Crawford told Josette that he'd be down on his knees praying until she called him back with good news.

Three hours later, Josette was beginning to feel numb. She had gone through so many varying emotions that her feelings stopped registering at all. The police department had erected a tent for the family members of the individuals trapped inside to sit. To ward off the chill that had settled in the late winter air, they had set up a few space heaters around the perimeter of the tent. Josette and Clint sat inside, sipping coffee and barely talking.

"Clint, you really don't have to wait here with

me. It's late and you've got to have other things to do," Josette said for about the tenth time.

"Josette, I'm not leaving you here alone," Clint repeated.

Josette sighed. It was hard to believe that just a few short hours ago she had been sitting inside of a café with Clint, explaining to him that although she and Seth were having problems, she had no intentions of straying from her marriage. The knowledge that, although faced with a proposition from this rather attractive man, she had had not one inkling of a desire to be disloyal to her husband or to her marriage, served to strengthen her faith that she and Seth would be okay. All they needed to do was make it through this crisis.

Josette looked around at the small crowd assembled in the tent. Ronni Blackwood, the wife of Ken Blackwood, a junior partner, was there. She had met Ronni several years ago at a partner-and-spouse golf outing and, while they hadn't seen much of one another over the years, she had always liked and respected the woman. Ronni was a councilwoman from the Bronx and as down-to-earth as you could get. Tonight, she and Josette had taken a few minutes away from the rest of the folks to talk softly, reassuring one another that their husbands would come out of this in one piece. Now, she was seated with her eldest son, who worked as a paralegal at the firm. Fortunately, he had already left the office for the evening when the gunman had arrived.

Also present were three young women whom Josette had not met before tonight. Their husbands or boyfriends were all associates with less than three years at the firm. In addition there was Martin Colfax, whose wife, Sherri, was a senior associate. Seth had told her that Sherri was up for partner and was a shoo-in. That would make her the first African-American female partner in the firm's history. Josette and Seth had had drinks with Martin and Sherri late in the summer, right around Seth's birthday.

From what they could tell, these were the only people who had a spouse or significant other in the office. However, since contact inside the offices had been fairly limited, it was impossible to say for sure if they had an accurate count. Fortunately, due to the late hour the gunman had chosen, many people had gone home for the day. Also, since he'd entered on a floor that was not the firm's main floor, other people had been able to safely evacuate the building.

By one o'clock in the morning, fatigue had set in and was beginning to work on the frayed ends of Josette's sanity. She'd laid her head down on her arms, which were folded on her knees. Clint was slouched over the folding table that held their coffee cups, exhausted as well. The tent was relatively silent, as most people were either resting or talking quietly to one another. A sudden burst of activity awoke them from their fragile slumber.

"What's going on?" Josette called out, jumping to her feet.

"Is it over?" called another anxious tent companion.

They rushed out of the tent and were greeted by Officer Patterson.

"Folks, listen up. We've got some encouraging news. The gunman has been talking to us and he's indicated that he wants to come out. We think that we will be seeing a positive end to this real soon."

A concerted murmuring of hope issued from the small crowd. Some of the anxious comrades reached out to hug one another, needing the human touch, mostly. Clint squeezed Josette's hand—the hand that he had been holding off and on for much of the night. Josette's breath remained caught in her throat, however. She was optimistic and apprehensive, yet she would not breathe deeply again until she saw her husband's face and heard his voice again.

That moment came thirty grueling minutes later. It seemed as if knowing the end was near made the time pass more slowly, more painstakingly than the prior torturous hours. Josette's eyes remained fixed to the glass revolving doors of the building, the activity surrounding them her only focal point.

When Seth walked out of the building, two police officers flanking him on either side, Josette could hardly contain herself. She let out an audible gasp, relief at seeing him flooding her body like making a mad dash through a waterfall. He was not wearing a coat nor suit jacket and his necktie was loose around his neck. He looked around at the sea of faces before him, searching it seemed. With his right hand, he gripped his left elbow. Blood leaked from his upper left arm, soaking through his ivory shirt. The officers cautiously led him to a waiting ambulance. Josette broke away from the officers blocking her and pushed aside one of the barricades with the force of a hurricane.

"Seth," she yelled. "Seth."

She ran to his side, throwing her arms around him when she reached him.

"Ma'am—"

"It's okay, let her ride with him," Officer Patterson, who had been gracious and accommodating throughout the night, said.

Josette kissed Seth's cheek, running her hands up and down the sides of his haggard face.

"Are you okay?" she asked.

Seth looked at his wife's tear-streaked face, the worry present on it only overshadowed by her love for him.

"I'm just fine, babe. I'm fine."

He used his good arm to pull her to him, determined that he would never let her go again. He had been a damned fool to jeopardize his marriage the way that he had, he knew. He also knew that God had given them a second chance, and he had no intentions of blowing it.

From a hundred or so feet away, Clint watched as Josette climbed into the ambulance beside her husband, never letting go of him. He smiled for them, although he felt sad for himself. Slowly, he backed away from the crowd, pulled the collar up on his coat and headed home alone.

Chapter 27

Josette slid the cheese, mushroom, onion and pepper omelet from the spatula expertly onto the white-and-flower-patterned plate. She placed three strips of perfectly fried bacon next to it. Finally, she buttered three slices of wheat toast, adding them to the plate and, along with a mug of coffee, dark and sweet, placed it all on a tray and carried it up the stairs.

"Good morning," she called as she pushed the bedroom door open with her behind.

Seth was just coming out of the bathroom. He was shirtless, clad in boxers, and a hand towel hung from his shoulder. His injured arm was wrapped with gauze and bandages, and was held in a sling. The bullet had entered his arm and lodged in a bone, causing a mild fracture. The doctor had successfully removed the bullet, but had informed him that he'd need to keep his arm immobile for the next few weeks.

"Hey, babe," he said, kissing Josette on the lips. "What's all this?"

"This is breakfast in bed for the hero. Now get back in it 'cause you're messing it up," she ordered.

She waited while Seth situated himself back on the bed before placing the tray on its legs over his lap.

"Mmm, mmm, mmm, this smells good," he said. "Dig in."

Josette sat at the foot of the bed, watching her husband devour his food. A chill ran up her spine as she thought about how close she had come to losing him. Seth had told her that the gunman, who'd turned out to be a thirty-five-year-old man with documented mental instabilities, had entered the office demanding to see his estranged wife. The woman, Gloria Jeffries, who was a dockets clerk at the firm, had only been working there for a few short months. She had left her prior job in an effort to escape her husband, who had spent the past six months in a mental institution. Despite the heightened security in place in Manhattan office buildings since September 11th, the gunman had been able to enter the elevator bank with a group of tenants going to another floor, eluding the sign-in process. Seth had approached the man at the reception desk. He was obviously upset and high on some type of drug. The receptionist had been cowering behind her desk, clearly terrified that the red-faced man would do more than scream at her. When Seth had asked the man to calm down and tell him what the problem was, he'd seemed to relax a bit. As he'd started to explain to Seth that all he wanted to do was to talk to Gloria for a minute, the receptionist had buzzed the alarm, which had alerted security to a problem. Two security officers had stepped off one of the elevators a minute later and at that point, undoubtedly feeling threatened, the man had pulled the gun out of his jacket. He'd pointed it at the unarmed security guards and Seth had immediately stepped in front of the irate man, still trying to calm him down.

Josette wanted to be angry with him for taking such a big chance, but she knew that that was the kind of man she'd married. While others had shrunk back in fear, Seth had swallowed his anxiety and had attempted to settle the situation positively. The man she loved could not step back and watch others face danger and not attempt to help. Once again, he'd made a connection with the man and it appeared to Seth that the man had been about to lower the gun and give himself up. Unfortunately, one of the guards had thought that moment was an opportunity to make a move on the suspect. Seth said that when the man had squeezed the trigger, he'd borne an expression of surprise, as if he'd been equally as caught off guard by the explosion as everyone else had been. The bullet had struck Seth, spinning him around, and the gunman had been instantly flustered. There'd been a brief struggle, but the man had been able to maintain control. He'd ushered Seth, the guards, the receptionist and a few other people who had assembled into the firm's library, where they'd spent the next few hours in uncertainty as to their futures.

Lost in thoughts that would continue to disturb her for a long time to come, Josette didn't realize that Seth had polished off her breakfast zealously. He moved the tray to the floor beside the bed and pulled Josette to him. Desire burned in his eyes as he smoothed her hair back from her face. His kiss was urgent, the intensity of it igniting her immediately. She returned his kiss, gratitude for the fact that he was still with her, alive and well, filling her to the brim.

Seth's hands roamed freely up and down her body. He wanted to touch every part of her as confirmation that he was still here and she was still his. The feel of his strong hand on the flesh of her behind, squeezing it and grinding it into his body, excited her, causing her breath to catch in her throat.

"Seth, your arm," Josette protested weakly.

"Don't worry about that. All you should be

thinking about is how good you feel," he whispered, his voice thick with passion.

Josette slid up farther onto the bed beside him. Seth freed her breasts from the red lace bra she wore, bending his head to kiss her nipples, one at a time. He flicked his tongue slowly across them, egged on by the sound of her breathing as it became ragged. He made circles around the outer circumference of her nipples, then zeroed in on the brown peaks. Finally, he opened his mouth fully, taking all of her in, sucking loudly, slurping at her nipples as she arched her back against him.

Her hands caressed the back of his head, fingering his curls. Despite having only one good arm to work with, Seth was doing magnificently. He moved away from her breasts, his tongue blazing a trail down her body to her stomach. Josette's legs parted without resistance when he reached her pubic region. He lapped softly at her opening, his hot breath sending ripples of pleasure through her body. When his tongue made contact with her clitoris, her body jerked as if doing a dance to its own music. Seth licked her, slowly at first and then faster as her juices began to flow. He looked up, loving the ecstasy-filled contortions on her face.

"Seth," she moaned, the sound of her husband's name on her tongue making her passion rise.

"Josette, baby, I love you," Seth answered.

He moved his face away from her hot oven, using his fingers in its place. He slid one then another into her, amazed that even after all of these years together there was still a tight, warm place waiting to receive him. He looked down at his wife as she moved her hips in demand against his hand, feeling like the luckiest man alive.

His throbbing manhood ached for her, and he knew that he could not wait one minute longer. Josette's moans were driving him wild as she begged for him to fill her up. He slid into her slowly, the friction of her walls almost too much for him to bear.

Josette rolled him over, climbing on top of him but never breaking their connection. He loved it when she took charge like that. With one hand on his chest and the other gripping the headboard, she eased herself up and down on his shaft, tightening the muscles of her vagina around him. Each time she moved, his instrument moved with her. He screamed. He couldn't help it. Later, he'd have to ask her where she'd learned that new trick, but right now he didn't care. All he knew was that if she kept on doing what she was doing, he would lose his mind.

They were both glad to know that their time apart had not taken away from the passion they'd found in the past few months. If anything, the separation served to spur them on to reach greater heights than ever before.

Lying in one another's arms afterward, both Seth and Josette knew that they had a lot to talk about before things would truly be back on track. However, they both agreed that if their lovemaking were any indication, they were definitely on their way.

They spent the weekend locked away in their home alone. After reassuring the rest of the family that Seth was fine and that he would recover from the gunshot wound with barely a scar as a remembrance, they used the opportunity to appreciate one another and the life they'd built together. Seth explained again, feeling that it was important that Josette truly understood, that he had never intended to have anything physical with the woman he'd been e-mailing. Josette made him understand that the verbal and mental betrayal was even more devastating to her. They explored the things they had both done wrong and dissected how each step they'd taken had moved them away from one another and off the path they'd laid together.

It was the first time that Seth had fully understood how important family was to Josette, which explained how difficult it had been for her to let the children go. He realized that he had been immature and selfish to feel jealous about the time she'd spent caring for the kids and taking care of the responsibilities of their home together. However, having her validate those feelings now made all the difference. She told him that she understood why he had been thrown for a loop when they'd discovered that she was pregnant. While it had been difficult to accept, she recognized that he had a right to feel that way and that it was understandable for him not to want to start child-rearing all over again at this point in his life. Seth expressed to Josette that the idea of her bearing his children had always filled him with pride and awe, but that his desire to have her all to himself had been so overwhelming that he couldn't see anything past that.

They both agreed that the best part of Seth being held hostage and shot was that it had forced them to face one another, face their fears and face themselves. While they'd always known exactly what they had in each other, it took the scare of a lifetime to impress upon them the importance of preserving it.

Chapter 28

After the turmoil and the triumphs of the past year, both Seth and Josette wanted their second honeymoon and twenty-first anniversary celebration to be special. Their original plans to travel to either the cluster of Hawaiian islands or to various spots in Europe did not speak to the essence of their beings as husband and wife, or to their successes as people of African descent. After much contemplation and discussion, they decided a trip to the origin of civilization was the only fitting place for them to begin the next phase of their lives together.

Their four-week trip to Africa began with a

grueling plane ride to Cape Town. They spent three days there, touring the wine lands of Stellenbosch. After being submersed in the utter beauty of the countryside, they set out for the next part of their African adventure. They boarded a luxury train at the foot of Table Mountain, on which they traveled for four days and nights in pampered splendor. Much of the time was spent talking to the workers on the train, whose vast knowledge of the country's history and culture was more enthralling than anything that could be read in a book.

Josette remarked that she did not ever want to get off the train, and Seth considered giving her what she wished for. He, too, felt as though those four days were the most refreshing and peaceful days he'd known in a long time. Yet as they coursed through the remainder of their extended trip, they realized that there was not much about the motherland that they did not find spiritually revitalizing.

They spent one night off the train in a deluxe Pretoria hotel near Capital Park. They stopped in the quaint Victorian village of Matjiesfontein, toured the historical mining town of Kimberley. Next they flew to Livingstone, located on the Zambian side of the majestic Victoria Falls. As beautiful as all of these venues were, they knew that a trip to the motherland would have been incomplete without an opportunity to view the slave castles of the Gold Coast. They flew to Ghana, where they spent the final week of their vacation visiting the slave castles where their ancestors had been stripped from their homeland and stuffed into waiting vessels that would take them to lands unknown.

The day before they were scheduled to depart, Seth gave Josette the surprise of her life. With the help of a local pastor, he'd arranged for them to renew their wedding vows. With the waves lapping against the rocks along the Atlantic shoreline of Cape Coast, Seth and Josette dedicated themselves to one another all over again.

"Nothing in life is guaranteed, which makes each reward all the more precious," Seth said as he held hands with the woman of his dreams.

Dressed in a simple, long, white cotton gown, her hair pinned up in an elegant bun and decorated with fragrant flowers, Josette was more beautiful to him in this historical surrounding than ever before.

"You are my reward, Josette, for believing in God and in love. He loved me so much that He placed you on my life's path to find. You make me want to be the best me that I can be and I promise you that for as long as we have together, I will do everything in my power to be the man that you deserve," Seth continued.

"Seth, the day I met you was the day that I under-stood my purpose in life. Finding you was no chance occurrence—it was God's plan for me. When I look into your eyes, I see a reflection of His love for me. We have built a life of happiness that many people never find, and I am so grateful for that opportunity. No matter what happens in the future, I know that I have truly loved. I love you with my whole soul, and I thank you for loving me with yours," Josette said, tears wetting her blushing cheeks.

Finally, things seemed to have gotten back on the right track in their lives. By the time they returned home, they felt as if there were nothing that they could not deal with, as long as they were together. As fate would have it, that faith was tested once again a short time later.

Despite his best efforts to scale back on his duties at the law firm, Seth became quite busy as soon as they returned. He began working long hours again, and Josette could see the toll it was taking on him. She gave him space, but that did not stop her from missing his touch as night after night passed with him working and her lying in bed dreaming about him.

"Maybe we've just been doing it too much," Seth said, his voice trembling with embarrassment. He rolled off Josette, sitting on the side of the bed with his back turned to her.

Josette leaned up on one elbow, the darkness preventing her from seeing her husband's disturbed face. It was the first night in a week that Seth had come to bed while she was still awake, and they'd found their way to one another in the dark. She placed one hand on his back and held it there for a moment.

"Seth," she said softly.

The sweetness and compassion in her voice compelled him to turn around to face her, even though he didn't want to see the ridicule he thought he would find in her eyes. He looked at his wife hesitantly, feeling like less of a man than he had in his entire life.

"What's wrong, baby?" she asked.

Even in the darkness of their bedroom, he could see that her eyes held nothing but love and understanding for him.

"I...I don't know. I want you, Josette.... Don't think for one minute that I don't. It's just...I... One minute it was there. I was all in it and it was feeling great and the next...I just lost it," Seth stammered.

"It's okay, Seth," she said. "It is," she insisted when he began shaking his head.

"I don't understand it."

"Seth, is there something on your mind...something going on that you haven't told me about?" Josette asked.

She had noticed that Seth had seemed a bit distracted lately. She knew that he was working hard and that he had been under a great strain at work, but she knew him well enough to know that it was more than that. While things were terrific between them, she sensed that he had a lot on his mind lately. She had been waiting patiently for him to either deal with whatever it was or to bring it to her. At least she could serve as his sounding board as usual, helping him to bounce around ideas until he worked it out. Up until this point, however, he had been keeping whatever it was bottled up inside of him.

"No, there's nothing—" Seth began and then stopped.

He looked at Josette and knew that there was no way he could sit there and lie to her face. Not after all they'd gone through. He took a deep breath.

"I've been having a problem at work," he said.

Josette regarded him for a moment.

"What kind of problem?"

"There's been an accusation…not really an accusation…more of a concern. Well, see, I don't really think it will amount to much, but—"

"Seth, stop going around the mountain and just get to the point. What is going on?"

She leaned over to the nightstand and turned the lamp on. A soft yellow glow bathed the room, exposing their nakedness, both physical and emotional. Josette's face was tight with apprehension as she listened to her husband. His bore a variety of emotions, the most prominent of which was fear.

"Remember the woman I was…I was e-mailing?"

Josette's heart stopped beating, or at least that was what it felt like to her. She wanted to get up and walk out of the room because there was no way she was about to sit there and listen to her husband tell her that he'd slept with that woman.

Seth saw the pained expression on her face and immediately knew what she was thinking.

"No, sweetie, it's nothing like that, I swear," he defended. He reached out, grabbed both her shoulders in his hands. "I swear it," he reaffirmed, looking deeply into her eyes.

Slowly the air began to move into and out of her lungs again. Seth waited until her eyes told him that she believed him before continuing.

"I promise you I have not had any contact with her since that day…the day you found out about it. I said I wouldn't and I haven't."

"So what's the problem, Seth?" Josette asked, having found her voice again.

"Well, as I told you, she works at a firm in Philadelphia…Bradley, Roth. They're a small investment-banking practice. They've got a pretty solid history, over twenty years in the business, and have worked with some of the largest corporate clients in the United States. Unfortunately, they have not been able to move past a certain point. Their small size limits them and frankly, it will take years for them to grow the firm to a size that would make them more competitive. Here's where we step in."

"I don't understand. We who?" Josette asked.

"We, meaning Waters, McLean, Berber and Crawford. We have been looking to expand our investment-banking department for a couple of years now and had even courted a few small firms out of New York and Atlanta. Those prospects didn't really pan out. Bradley, Roth, however, is the ideal size, we have a strong working relationship with them and we have already been outsourcing some work for many of our clients with them. It's a sweet deal for both sides. Their head partners would come on as junior partners with us, we've assured spaces for all of their legal staff and a good number of the support staff. Those whose positions would not be transferable would be assisted in finding other comparable employment and given generous severance pay."

"It sounds like a win-win situation, Seth. I don't understand what the problem is."

"Well, I realized from an ethical standpoint that my relationship with that woman, Vivian King is her name…well, it could be construed incorrectly if people found out about it. I mean, she would now be a member of my firm and direct subordinate to me. She's one of the partners who would be brought on as a midlevel partner and that could be construed as improper given that she and I have somewhat of a history."

There, he'd said it. Seth watched as Josette processed the information he'd just given her, and he knew that he was asking a lot of his wife to be understanding and sympathetic to his plight right now. Their love had been revitalized and renewed, but still he knew that even the best of marriages exist on a fragile balance. With the exception of this recent indiscretion, he had always been loyal to Josette. He had also prided himself on being honest with her and not keeping things from her. However, he had wanted to spare her knowing that his stupid mistakes of a few months ago had not only damaged their marriage, but had also potentially damaged his professional reputation.

"Have you spoken to anyone about this?"

"Yes. Walt and I talked it over, off the record of course, and he, too, recognizes it as a potential problem. If she comes onboard and makes any sort of waves, this could come back to haunt me. Alternatively, there is no way we could not extend a job offer to her. First, because she's a damned good attorney with an impeccable record. There would be no grounds for not bringing her in along with the merger. Secondly, even if we did find a way around that, she would not take that lying down."

Walter Berber and Seth had been more than colleagues and partners for the past twenty years. They had become friends. They shared a special relationship that did not exist between them and the other partners, often confiding in one another on a variety of issues. Josette held her tongue as she struggled with the burning question of why Seth hadn't talked out his issues with Walt in the first place, thereby avoiding the entire situation with little miss e-mail pal. However, for the health and progress of their relationship, she didn't say that.

"So what does Walt suggest?"

"He thinks that I should tell the other partners, both current and those over at Bradley, Roth. That way, nothing can be construed as being in an underhanded fashion."

"And what do you think about that?" Josette asked.

"I don't think I really have any other choices. I can't believe this." Seth sighed.

He looked at Josette again, wanting her pity even though he knew that he didn't deserve it.

"I'm sorry, Josie. I know this is all my fault.... I was stupid, and I didn't think. I'm sorry that this is happening now."

"Seth, I don't think we need to rehash all of that. What's done is done. I've forgiven you and I've moved on. What we need to do now is figure out how to stop a bad situation from getting worse."

Seth reached over and pulled Josette to him. Her body relaxed against his as he stroked her back.

"I'm glad you said *we,*" he whispered into her hair.

"It is *we,* Seth. If we always remember to come to one another when we are in need of anything, we will be all right."

"I know. I know."

"Right now, Seth, you've got to stop letting this eat at you. I know you're worried about your reputation and that of the firm, but you can't let it plague you like this."

"I'm sorry. I know it's not fair to you."

"You're right about that. I'm getting used to your good loving so I'm going to need you to be in tip-top shape." Josette laughed.

"You know I aim to please," Seth said. "Tell you what. Even if my little soldier ain't up to the task, I'm sure I can think of other ways to start a war up in here," he said suggestively.

They were all talked out for the night, as Seth used his imagination to satisfy his wife. Ironically, simply sharing his problems with his wife served to lift much of what was burdening his body.

Chapter 29

Marcus pulled into the driveway slowly, trying to avoid making any noise. Having been given a pass from his political-science professor for his final exam due to the fact that he had been able to maintain an *A* average, Marcus had finished the semester and was home for summer break a day early. He had been so eager to get there and surprise his parents that he had driven for longer stretches of time without resting. Despite having thoroughly enjoyed his newfound freedom and independence by attending a college so far away from home, he missed his parents more than he thought he would. He was looking forward to home-cooked meals, helping his mom out in the kitchen and kicking it with his father.

At shortly before six o'clock in the morning, Marcus arrived. He fully expected that his parents would still be in bed asleep at this hour on a Saturday morning. Using his key, he slipped into the house, stifling his giggles as he thought about how surprised and happy his mother would be when she saw him. He climbed the stairs and stole down the corridor until he reached the end where the master bedroom was located. He peered inside the open door and found that his parents' bed was empty. Puzzled, he turned to retrace his steps, but before he could move, he heard a sound. He moved into his parents' room and realized that their bathroom door was closed. Curiosity overruling his senses, Marcus walked over to the door and realized that the sound he'd heard was soft laughter. He placed his ear against the door, his fist paused to knock when the sounds became more distinct and clear. He covered his mouth with his hand and backed away from the door, out of the bedroom and down the corridor.

Marcus sat down on the top step of the circular stairwell, dumbfounded. He was completely embarrassed and relieved that they had not known he was there. Torn between going into his bedroom and shutting the door or re-entering the house and making as much noise as possible, he could not fathom what to do. He dialed Simone, who was still down at Stockton and would not come home until the middle of next week. After she laughed in his ear for a full minute, she advised him to retrace his steps, get back in his truck, drive away and come back in a few hours. She did not seem at all disturbed by the news that he'd just caught their parents making love—loudly at that.

"Marcus, they're human, duh? I mean, wasn't Mom just pregnant a few months ago?" Simone chuckled.

"I know. That's exactly what I'm talking about. What if she gets knocked up again? Ew, this is gross," he whispered.

"Marcus, knock it off. How in the hell do you think your big head got here? They're grown. So what you need to do is get your butt out of their house so they can have their privacy. You don't want to get caught in the house when they come out of there, do you? Talk about embarrassing," Simone chided.

Marcus realized that some of what his sister was saying had merit. He sprang off the step and headed downstairs, face aflame. Although he did not know it at the time, Marcus would have a lot to get used to. For starters, it seemed that he was home more than his parents were now. They were constantly out and about, taking short weekend trips, and doing other things that didn't include him. At first, Marcus was not sure that he liked this change of circumstances. There seemed to be some imbalance in the orderly home life he had come to expect. Simone, on the other hand, was quite relieved that her parents had become inseparable, giggling lovers again. The tension that had developed around the baby had not gone unnoticed by her and despite the fact that she was an adult, the idea of her parents divorcing made her sick to her stomach. Eventually, and with Simone's assistance, Marcus came to accept the new Mr. and Mrs. Crawford, as if he'd had a choice.

"Come on, babe, it's time to get up. You said you couldn't sleep past ten," Seth said, shaking Josette gently.

"Mmm," Josette moaned. "Ten more minutes."

"Nope, now. Come on, Josie, you've got a million things to do," Seth said.

He knew that if he allowed Josette to sleep a minute longer, as much as he wanted her to get her rest, she would have his head later on. While he, like her, would love to sleep this particular day away, it was not an option. He kissed Josette's cheek and neck, and slowly she began to rouse. She reached up, lacing one arm around his neck and pulling him down to her.

"Can't we just stay in bed?" she whispered.

Josette nibbled on Seth's ear. When she slipped her tongue inside, he pulled away slightly.

"Woman, don't start that," Seth said, his tone unconvincing.

Josette sat up in the bed, resting her back against the headboard.

"I cannot believe I let Carmelita snow me into this one," she complained.

"I can't believe it, either, but you did," Seth replied.

"Gee, thanks honey. Way to make me feel better."

"Well, you said it first. Look, let's just make the best of the situation. She's your baby sister and she just got married—"

"Again," Josette answered snidely.

"Josette."

"No, Seth. I mean, really. This amounts to her third trip down the aisle. We haven't even met this man—no one in the family has. All we know is that he's from Connecticut originally, and he moved out to Arizona with his wife three years ago, but he's now divorced. He was self-employed, but now he's out of work due to a back injury. He's been living with Carmelita for the past year and for all intents and purposes, she's supporting them. Oh, and did I mention that the man has a criminal record? Mom told me that. What exactly are we celebrating here?"

"Josie, aren't you the one who's always saying 'to each his own'? As much as we disapprove, we can't judge her. You never know—this guy might be the one."

"Whatever. All I know is that I don't understand why his family isn't throwing this little shindig."

"We're doing it because your sister asked you to do it and you can't refuse her. So go ahead and moan and groan. Get it out of your system and then let's get busy."

Josette regarded Seth for a moment, and then, like a spoiled child, she pushed back the covers and climbed out of bed. Seth smacked her behind as she walked past him.

Once Josette had showered and dressed, she felt slightly better, although she still was not pleased about the current circumstances. She loved Carmelita dearly but she could not understand why her sister was so impulsive. Their mother had always cautioned them about taking their time to make informed decisions. Both of their parents were stable, hardworking people. They followed the rules, went to church every Sunday without fail and lived their lives in service to their community and to God. They had always impressed upon their kids the importance of planning and making wise choices. Josette and Bernardo took their lessons to heart. Carmelita, however, had always been a loose cannon. She had refused to go to college, deciding to take a job at a trendy taco bar. She'd met a man after working there for only two weeks, and two months later she'd married him.

Josette knew that it was against her religious and moral beliefs to stand in judgment of another human being, but that didn't stop her from worrying about her sister. Despite her misgivings, however, she had agreed to throw this reception for her sister's third, and hopefully final, marriage. Carmelita had maintained some friendships in the New York area when she'd lived here for a few years in between her first and second marriages. Since her new husband was originally from Connecticut, all of his family and friends resided in the area. As a result, it had been decided that this would be the ideal location.

Josette had hoped that their parents could fly out for the party, but they had declined, citing Lourdes's recent troubles with her asthma and Benjamin's back as reasons for why they weren't up for the trip at this point. Josette suspected that like her, they were dismayed by Carmelita's haphazard lifestyle and didn't really feel like celebrating this latest occurrence.

Josette spent the morning shopping. She purchased a case of champagne, several bottles of rum, gin, vodka, tonic and mixers. It took the liquorstore clerk three trips to load everything into her car. At the flower shop, Josette purchased various arrangements to decorate the house. Two and a half hours later, she was back at home and Seth had turned their already orderly house into a spotless, decorated party palace.

Marcus had returned home from his early morning workout at the gym. He and Seth removed all of Josette's purchases from the car, carrying them into the dining room as instructed. Josette spent the next hour cutting and organizing what amounted to twelve vases of flowers. Once the arrangements were done to her satisfaction, she placed them in strategic places around her home.

The dinner was to be catered by Clementine's, a small soul-food place in White Plains. The menu Josette had decided upon included a cheese-and-fruit platter, catfish bites, pan-seared shrimp wrapped in crispy bacon, and barbecued pork skewers as appetizers. Barbecued baby-back spareribs, baked turkey wings and stewed snapper would follow, along with a variety of side dishes. Finally, Josette had personally baked the carrot and rum cakes for desert. Simone's contribution was a beautiful arrangement of fruit sorbet, which she'd decorated with fruits cut in the shape of hearts.

By the time the guests had begun to arrive, Josette was in a better mood. The groom actually seemed to be a nice man and her sister, Carmelita, had never been more radiant. The groom's family were an okay bunch, with the exception of his nephew, Oscar, who drank too much and turned out to be a sloppy drunk. He followed Simone around all night long, asking her out and refusing to take no for an answer until Connor gripped him by the forearm and had a little chat with him. Seth discreetly interceded, preventing the altercation from becoming a knock-down, drag-out fight, and the remainder of the night went smoothly.

The party served as a reminder to Josette of how

fortunate she was. Her sister had spent years trying to find her life partner and had gone through years of drama, which she would never be able to recover. Josette had been lucky enough to find Seth early on and, despite the fact that at times they'd faltered, they had never failed.

None of the Crawfords could have predicted how much different their lives would be a year ago. Everything that had happened to them had been a test of their faith. With Josette's support and counsel, Seth worked out the precarious situation with his firm's pending merger, and saved his reputation and that of the firm. When the opportunity of a lifetime arose for Seth, it was because of their renewed faith in each other that he and Josette jumped on it without hesitation. The firm had recently developed a growing practice in Milan, Italy. So much so, that it was decided to expand the firm to include offices in that locale. Seth's partners decided that due to his expertise and savvy, Seth would be the only logical choice to spearhead the development and start-up of that office. Before he could completely consider all of the implications of such a huge move and his abilities to get it done, Josette had begun making arrangements for them to go.

"I believe in you," she said, kissing him deeply with love coating every word.

That was all Seth needed to hear to know that he could and would take on the daunting task of establishing a new office. He accepted the challenge and they prepared to depart for Milan with the expectation of having to remain there for six to nine months.

Josette took a leave of absence from New Hope, appointing Natalie as interim director and hiring two new staff members to fill the need that her departure would create. Everything else happened in a whirlwind, giving them little time to digest it all. The kids were both ecstatic, looking forward to getting to spend Christmas break in Italy. The timing for this new adventure could not have been better for them to seize the opportunity. Josette's brother, Bernardo, had decided that he wanted to take a short break from traveling and at the start of the summer had accepted a temporary reassignment in the department of facilities management, which would keep him local for the coming months. He took them up on their request to move into the house to take care of things for them in their absence. At the beginning of August, the furnishings and other items that they'd wanted to take with them were shipped ahead and, in turn, some things of Bernardo's—who was scheduled to return from visiting their parents in California the week after Seth and Josette's departure—had been delivered a couple of days ago.

Simone was beginning her junior year and had opted to move into her own apartment off campus. It was agreed that it would be better for Lady, the family's aging golden retriever, not to travel to Milan with Seth and Josette, but to be taken in by Simone in New Jersey. Josette did not entertain one moment of worry or concern for Simone because she realized that her daughter was indeed the responsible, intelligent young woman whom Josette had set out to raise. Despite what Simone said to the contrary, Josette also knew intuitively that her daughter had found the love of her life in Connor and that the two of them would be headed toward something permanent very soon. Neither Josette nor Seth could be happier, finding Connor to be a better future son-in-law than they could have asked for.

Seth had initially worried that Josette would find it difficult to leave Marcus behind, but to his surprise, she was absolutely all right with it. Marcus was doing well in Florida and was even more excited about his sophomore year after he'd decided to switch majors to pre-law, desiring to follow in his father's footsteps. The apron string had finally been cut and Josette watched with pride and excitement as her son headed back to school and to the life he was building down there for himself.

The night before they were scheduled to leave, Seth and Josette begged out of going to dinner with their neighbor, Phil, and his new girlfriend as planned. They decided that they wanted to spend their last night alone in their home. As they took their final check around the house, neither could avoid the feelings of nostalgia that came over them. Although the plan was to remain in Milan for only a period of six to nine months, they realized that there was a strong possibility that structuring the new offices could take longer or they could very well fall in love with their temporary home and decide to stay. The past year had taught them both to be open to all of the possibilities of life because there was really no other way to truly live.

Josette prepared a simple dinner of pot roast and potatoes. Seth lit the candles and poured the wine. Before they sat down to eat, however, their eyes met and each caught the smoldering signal that proceeded to consume them both. Dinner grew cold.

Second chance for romance...

When
Valentines
Collide

Award-winning author

ADRIANNE
*B*YRD

Therapists Chante and Michael Valentine agree to a "sex-therapy" retreat to save their marriage. At first the seminar revives their passion—but their second chance at love is threatened when a devastating secret is revealed.

"Byrd proves again that she's a wonderful storyteller."
—*Romantic Times BOOKreviews* on *The Beautiful Ones*

*Available the first week of February,
wherever books are sold.*

KIMANI™
ROMANCE

*A dramatic story of danger and adventure
set in the depths of Africa...*

IN THE LIGHT of LOVE

Bestselling Arabesque author

Deborah Fletcher Mello

Working together in a war-torn African nation where danger
lurked everywhere, Talisa London and Dr. Jericho Becton
were swept up in a wave of desire that left them breathless.
But would they survive their mission with their love—
and lives—intact?

Available the first week of February, wherever books are sold.

KIMANI™
ROMANCE

www.kimanipress.com

Essence bestselling author

DONNA HILL

If I Were Your
Woman

The second story in the Pause for Men *miniseries.*

A messy affair left Stephanie Moore determined
to never again mix business with pleasure. But her
powerful attraction to Tony Washington has her
reconsidering—even though she suspects Tony may be
married. She'll need the advice of her Pause for Men
partners to help her sort out her dilemma.

Pause for Men—four fabulously fortysomething divas
rewrite the book on romance.

*Available the first week of February,
wherever books are sold.*

KIMANI™
ROMANCE

www.kimanipress.com

USA TODAY bestselling author

BRENDA JACKSON

The third title in the Forged of Steele miniseries...

Beyond Temptation

Sexy millionaire Morgan Steele will settle for nothing less than the perfect woman. And when his arrogant eyes settle on sultry Lena Spears, he believes he's found her. There's only one problem—the lady in question seems totally immune to his charm!

Only a special woman can win
the heart of a brother—
Forged of Steele

**Available the first week of January
wherever books are sold.**

KIMANI™
ROMANCE

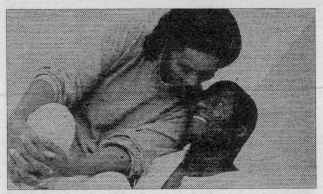

Celebrate Valentine's Day with this collection of heart-stirring stories...

Love in Bloom

"These three authors have banded together to create some excellent reading."
—Romantic Times BOOKreviews

FRANCINE CRAFT,
LINDA HUDSON-SMITH,
JANICE SIMS

Three beloved Arabesque authors bring romance alive in these captivating Valentine tales of first love, second chances and promises fulfilled.

Available the first week of January wherever books are sold.